ALL HE LEFT BEHIND

BOOKS BY CLARK

THE STAINS OF TIME

The Piano of Death

The Boot of Destiny

The Chains of Desire

The Elixir of Denial

The Dance of Dreams

OTHER BOOKS

Those Little Bastards

All He Left Behind

Missing Mr. Wingfield

The Seven Wives of Silver

Bad Poetry Night

Out of the Woods

Under the World

ALL HE LEFT BEHIND

E. CHRISTOPHER CLARK

Published in the United States by Clarkwoods in Chelmsford, Massachusetts.

ISBN for the Print Edition: 978-1-952044-02-1
ISBN for the Digital Edition: 978-1-952044-03-8

Library of Congress Control Number: 2010910814

CONTENTS

For my girls, Kaylee and Melody; my wife, Stephanie; and in memory of my father-in-law Stephen Woodsum and my friend Susan Bullock

THE SEVENTH DRAFT

C all me Ishmael. Or call me Lolita, for that matter. For though I shudder to think of myself as ever having been the light of someone's life, I am certain that I have borne responsibility for the fire burning in someone's loins. A great many someones, if I may be so bold. So, go ahead and call me a joker, call me a fool. Because, right at this moment, I'm totally cool. Clear as a crystal, sharp as a knife, I feel like I'm in the prime of my... Well, you get the point.

It was the best of times, it was the worst of times, and once upon a midnight dreary, while I pondered weak and weary, I asked aloud, "When shall we three meet again—in thunder, lightning, or in rain?" And then a vagrant in the street turned her head and answered me, "When the hurlyburly's done, when the battle's lost and won."

I had a dream, I tell you! I had a dream where I told thousands of Germans that I was a jelly donut—*Ich bin ein Berliner!* I had a dream that I was not a crook, that there would be—Read my lips!—no new taxes. I had a dream that I was back in Berlin, asking Mr. Gorbachev to tear down the wall; that our American values were not luxuries, but necessities—not the salt on our bread, but the bread itself. I had a dream that our long national nightmare was over. But it's never over, friend, not this one.

I place my left hand on the Bible, raise my right, and repeat after you, "I swear to tell the truth, the whole truth, and nothing but the truth, so help me God." So, help me, God. Help me!

My name is Matthew Silver, and I am an alcoholic.

...and I am a nymphomaniac.

...and, at this point, on the seventh draft of this monstrosity whose pages you are leafing through ever faster, searching for *the* point, I have so little faith in my ability to construct a complete sentence that I must resort to cheap parlor tricks of language. I must pillage the words of others, remix them, and flip the script, if you will.

But leave me to my own devices, take away my bookshelves and leave me with a composition notebook and a box of sharpened number twos, and see what happens.

...

Nothing, and a whole lot of it.

But I'll try again, of course. Because I am a writer. And this is what I do.

THE TALE OF OLD SILAS

The most troubling thing about his nightmare was that it never ended the same way twice. If there had been some sense of continuity, some sticky end he could anticipate with dread each time, then it might have been easier to bear. But, no. One night it was the simple, profound pain of seawater flooding his lungs; the next it was a great white whale swallowing him whole; and the night after that it'd be the plank, walking the plank and plunging into the embrace of the shark below, feeling his flesh torn asunder, watching his foot and his boot float off toward the shore. Yes, the conclusion was revised each night, the only common theme his untimely demise. Which was what made this night's version all the more troubling. In this one, he didn't die.

Silas sat up in his bed in the attic of the old colonial, its drafty windows clattering in the strong winds of a November gale. He drew the thick wool blanket tightly around himself, hoping that, like the armor of Achilles, it would protect him from all comers. But still he shivered. Still, he wept. Now that he'd pulled it up over his head, there wasn't enough blanket left to cover his ankles, his heels.

The ninth to bear the name, Silas Odysseus Silver was the first of that long line to fear the sea; the rest of them had actually worked it, had actually made their names as the pilots of English, and now American, sailing vessels. But the trade was already at the beginning of its steady decline on Cape Cod; by the dawn of the next century—the *twentieth*—most of the business would move north to Cape Ann, *our* cape's rocky, inhospitable cousin. His brothers-in-law, once commanders of the grandest of ships, and travelers to exotic ports of call—they had traveled as far as Canton and the Sandwich Islands—would soon be reduced to cultivating the lowly cranberry. Thus, there was no need for a young man who actually shrunk at the sight of the slippery seduc-tress he was meant to tame, not time anymore to wait for someone like Silas to overcome his particular psychosis. Maybe in some other, earlier age. But not now.

Rain lashed against his window, like a vengeful sprite trying to force its way in. The boot, the boot, the boot. It all came back to the boot. For the boot had been there this time. But not like before, not like before. Because he wasn't in the jaws of the shark this time as he watched the boot borne off on the waves—this time the embrace was far warmer, far more...

He was an infant when it happened, the incident with the boot. Too young to remember the details of it himself, he knew the story only through the lens of his sisters' own fractured memories; their mother refused to speak of it. And perhaps it was worse, knowing the story only this way, knowing only with the distant and often contradictory embellishments of three young women who were barely old enough to remember that day themselves.

Silas shook harder beneath the blanket now, so vivid was the horror inherent in his vision of that fateful day.

It was in the twilight of 1844 that his family's own twilight began in earnest, a blustery December morning that brought two fellows down from the very tip of Cape Cod—Provincetown—

through the snowy streets of humble Harwich. Silas was in the arms of his mother, and, along with his sisters, watched, from the window above the kitchen sink, the two men trudging through the freshly fallen snow, the wind whipping off of Nantucket Sound so fiercely that it nearly toppled them and their terrible burden. They carried with them a burlap sack containing all that was left of his father—a boot which had washed ashore, into the dunes that ringed the Race Point lighthouse, and within that boot a severed foot clod in a tattered stocking, stitched with the poor man's initials in the sole.

While his sisters served the weary travelers tea and biscuits, it was said that Silas himself, a mere babe, could not take his eyes off of the stocking—minus the foot now, of course. He pointed at it, and struggled to wriggle from his mother's arms to touch the object of his newfound obsession. But he would never touch it, just as he would never again feel the rough, stubbled face of his father pressed against his cheek in a silent farewell before heading out to sea. The sock and the boot would be burned. And the foot —well, nobody could remember what had happened to the foot (or, at least, nobody would say), but Silas suspected that it had been burned, too, whatever small part of it there was, for the smell of burning flesh, no matter if it were the flesh of a pig, or a cow, or a lamb, still churned his stomach to this day. Even the smell of his own sweat, his own skin after a day in the sun raising a barn or a house—even that was enough to make him sick.

His stomach churned now, somewhere beneath the dark folds of the blanket, at the thought of he and his love basking under the noon-day sun on that distant shore he had dreamt for them, she paying no attention to the bandaged stump at the end of his left leg, where his foot had once been, as she asked him, "Do you love me?"

"O heaven," he moaned as she ran her hand down along his chest, along his stomach. Down, down, down. "O heaven, o earth, bear witness to this sound, and crown what I profess with kind event if I speak true! If hollowly, invert what best is boded me to mischief! I, beyond all limit of what else I' th' world, do love, prize, honor you."

And how she cried then, thick sobs punctuating her speech as she said, "I am fool to weep at what I am glad for."

"Wherefore weep you?"

"At mine unworthiness, that dare not offer what I deserve to give, and much less take what I shall die to want. But this is trifling; and all the more it seeks to hide itself, the bigger bulk it shows. Hence, bashful cunning, and prompt me, plain and holy innocence! I am your wife, if you will marry me; if not, I'll die your maid. To be your fellow you may deny me; but I'll be your servant whether you will or no."

"My mistress dearest. And I thus humble ever."

"My husband then?"

"Ay, with a heart as willing as bondage e'er of freedom. Here's my hand."

"Ay, but where is your foot?"

"My foot, my foot, my kingdom for a foot!"

And that was how it ended this night, his terrible dream. For all the world truly was a stage, and they merely players. But he was no Ferdinand to her Miranda, no matter how often they read the play together. No, he was the boatswain and this was his exit. Forever would he have the dream, but never would he have the lady.

This was his exit, his terrible exit. He stared out from under the blanket, across the dark blue murk of his room. "Oh, I am fortune's fool," he said to himself then. "I am fortune's fool." Closing his eyes, he thought to himself that he would much rather have seen the terrible dream through to its inevitable conclusion than to be facing the waking nightmares which were plaguing him now, the visions of musket fire piercing his arms, his chest, of a cannon ball taking his legs out from under him. The thought of his last words, of his fellow soldier holding him in his arms, clutching him to his breast, whispering, "Courage, man. The hurt cannot be much."

And his reply, "No, 'tis not so deep as a well, nor so wide as a church door; but 'tis enough, 'twill serve. Ask for me tomorrow and you shall find me a grave man."

୧ᢤ୨

OF COURSE, yes, all of this is conjecture—I'm making it up; I couldn't possibly know what this ancestor of mine was thinking on the day he took his leave of Harwich and made his way off of the Cape to do his duty, to serve his country. I've had to build this scene from precious little evidence, but I think it does the man justice, even in its more melodramatic moments.

Little is known of the younger days of the man who would be the last Silas Silver. In his later years, he became a man of few words and of much disdain for the company of others. To paint a picture of his youth we must rely on a single photograph, taken the day before he and the rest of the 24th Massachusetts Infantry departed for Annapolis, 9 December 1861, and his well-documented obsession with the works of the Elizabethan playwright William Shakespeare, a contemporary of the last man in the Silver line not to be called Silas. Aside from the fact that most of the few words the old man spoke in his later years were cribbed directly from the Bard, there is the surviving collection of Shakespearean drama which is the pride of our family's library to this day. The pages of those old volumes are dog-eared and riddled with the chicken-scratch of our Victorian ancestor, and they betray a truly all-encompassing obsession with the work.

The photograph betrays that he not only knew of tragedy in a literary sense, but that he had experienced it in his own life, as well. Reflected in his eyes, which are cast off to the left, avoiding the steady gaze of the foreboding contraption about to steal away forever a part of himself that he wasn't sure he was ready to give up, a careful observer will see an overwhelming sadness, and a sense of resignation at the hand that fate has dealt him. In the slouch of his shoulders one might identify the weight of his family's good name bearing down upon him, the weight of obligation. And in the tentative grasp of his hands around the musket, how could you not see doubt and fear?

Microfilmed copies of the town records of Harwich confirm that there must have been a young lady on his mind at the time of his enlistment. Silas and his sweetheart, Tamson O'Rourke, had filed their intent to marry just weeks before Silas's enlistment. But no record of the marriage can be found. Indeed, the next documented evidence of Tamson O'Rourke is her death record, filed in the waning years of the war. She died in Boston, of consumption, and, according to the record, had never been married. Her occupation—actress—was not common in the puritanical Beantown of the mid-nineteenth century. A check of the newspapers of the time, and of available programs and posters, finds no record of any headlining performance, but it is possible that she worked under an assumed name.

What is certain in all this uncertainty is that she was actually more than Silas's sweetheart. She was also his cousin, his *first* cousin.

So it's not hard to imagine why this romance, which had probably gone further than the old Widow Silver would have liked, was never consummated. It's not hard to imagine that Silas's enlistment in the Union army was a convenient way to get him away from that hopeless dreamer of a girl, the daughter of the family's black sheep and her worthless Irish husband. It's not hard to paint a picture, our grandfather used to tell us, when the palette you've been given is so vast, and so full of possibility.

So, Silas went off to fight in the war of the rebellion, torn from a girl whom he loved deeply for all the reasons his mother loathed her. A tale as old as time, song as old as rhyme: Beauty and a man who would soon become a beast. The 24th Massachusetts Infantry was involved in both decisive victories and losses in and around the harbor of Charleston, South Carolina. In February of 1862, they took the strategic point of Roanoke Island, assaulting the forts along its narrow waist in a victory that helped tighten the blockade of the rebel city considerably. But they lost just as decisively in Secessionville in June of that year. All wars, I suppose, are like a yo-yo—the incessant back and forth—but when you're fighting yourself, as our country was then, it seems to me that the fruitless nature of it all could only be more amplified. Punch your own arm and sure, there is a momentary sense of triumph, but then there's the pain, and pain, in my experience, lingers for far longer than pleasure. Soon they would be engaging in useless displays of machismo, burning the stockpiled grain of the enemy in July of 1864. And, not long after that, receiving what later generations of American soldiers would call a million dollar wound, Silas the Ninth would be discharged and sent back home, back into the bosom of an old widow who was drawing her last breaths.

The last of the Silver males, Silas was charged with the propagation of the family name. It was the dying wish of old Widow Silver that the ninth Silas Silver make it his life's mission to beget the tenth. And Silas, well aware by now that his long lost love was truly lost, made up his mind to remove love from the equation. He set out to find his bride with the same sense of blind, systematic determination with which he had tackled the collected works of Shakespeare.

He married first, in 1865, the only daughter of a local cranberry baron, a girl named Patience, who did little but try his. When she succumbed to influenza five years later without providing him his heir, he married again. And when that woman did nothing but steal away two decades of his life before catching her death of cold, he married again. And again. For one wife, once a woman of ill-repute, who claimed to be half-Wampanoag, he tore down his mother's home, which his bride claimed was beset upon by evil spirits, and built in its place a sprawling, garish Victorian that left so little land exposed on the property that you couldn't properly call it a lawn. And though he had bedded her in every one of its eleven rooms, only his libido had been sated, never his desire for a son.

It was in the summer of 1913, just six months shy of his seventieth birthday, that Silas Silver met Annie O'Reilly, the teenage daughter of Irish immigrants, whose sparkling green eyes, from across the room, seemed to reflect the one aspect of old Silas that women of all ages still found attractive. Widows and spinsters who had lived long enough to know both women would note in their journals the more than passing resemblance that the young Miss O'Reilly bore to the long dead Tamson O'Rourke. And one must assume that that resemblance was at least one reason why the shriveled organ of Silas's heart may have begun to beat more strongly than it had in years.

They met at a barn dance, that bastion of the Cape Cod social scene. And it was Mister O'Reilly, not his daughter, who made the first move, making his way across the dance floor with a proposition for the entranced Mister Silver.

"I see you fancy my daughter there, Mister Silver," said Mister O'Reilly, smiling, clapping Silas on the shoulder. "And I hear you've a desire to spread your seed, as it were."

"This is quite a vulgar conversation, sir," Silas grunted, turning to leave. "Now, if you'll excuse me..."

Mister O'Reilly grabbed hold of Silas by the shoulders then and held him steady, seething in a near-whisper. "My daughter's borne the bastards of no less than three of this town's less-than-desirable sons. I have no room left in my home for any more and no explanations left for how my wife continues to bear children even as her hair grows more silver than a storm cloud. If you would be so kind as to help us alleviate our financial burden, I would consent to offer you my daughter's hand."

And so it was that Silas Silver came to marry his seventh wife, the young Miss Annie O'Reilly. And so it was that, in the spring of the year 1914, Silas's wish for an heir was finally granted. At Annie's wishes, because she claimed the name Silas was now "out of fashion," they named the child Elijah. "A good Christian name," Annie said. Ten months later, before dying in the delivery room, she gave him a second child, Dorothy. Dottie, for short.

In some earlier age, perhaps Silas would have been a passable single father. But things had changed, as things are apt to do, and Silas not only couldn't empathize with his children; he couldn't understand them, either. Elijah took up, not the professions of his cousins—lawyers, politicians, and bankers all—but became, instead, little more than a traveling minstrel, blowing on his horn wherever it took him. He eschewed the classics in favor of dime novels, hornswaggled his way out of the second Great War while his cousins bled to death on the beaches of Normandy, then courted and married some poor Polack's daughter.

And the girl was even worse, living the life of a harlot, calling herself an *artist*, living in sin with one man after another until finally, in the fall of 1944, she got what she deserved—consumption—and found herself, like her father down the Cape, shivering beneath the covers of the last bed she would ever sleep in.

Elijah came to Silas then, in his bed at the Cape Cod hospital in Hyannis, to plead for Dottie's dying wish—a spot in the family plot in Harwich. "All she wants is to be next to Mum. It doesn't have to be..."

Silas cackled between hacking and wheezing and he said to his son, "You'd sooner catch a weasel asleep than convince me to allow that strumpet's corpse to pollute the eternal resting place of my family."

"I should never have come," said Elijah, heading for the door. "Dottie thought that age might have softened you, but I can see that, even after a century spent on this Earth, you're still a no good son of a bitch."

"I would live a hundred more years," Silas screamed at his

retreating son, at that coward, that dog, "if only to see that the two of you never tarnish my family's good name... A PLAGUE ON BOTH YOUR HOUSES!" he screamed, through the phlegm that was nearly suffocating him.

But Elijah, the man would become my grandfather, had never read Shakespeare. He didn't get the reference. And he would leave his father's room that day thinking that the old man had simply gone mad.

Which, in a way, he had.

The last Silas Silver would not live another hundred years. He died that autumn, just after his daughter. And his attendant would make a call north that day, to summon that last scion of the Silver family south for the funeral, a call eerily similar to the one I would have to make some fifty years later.

METAL NIGHT AT THE ROLLER KINGDOM

Michael Silver was in love with Desiree Emerson, or at least that's what he told himself. At fourteen, maybe he didn't know exactly what love was—his cousin Matt was telling him as much over the phone right now—but he knew for sure that he felt something for Desiree. He didn't just have the hots for her. As his grandfather had so eloquently put it, at a Christmas party back in the day, back before his family's Great Schism, back when friends and family crowded the halls of their Cape house on every possible occasion, Michael lit up like Rudolph's nose at the mere sight of Desiree. And if that wasn't love, then what the heck was it?

What was it about Desiree that made her so combustible? Well, you had to look at it this way: she was a senior, and a cheerleader, and far prettier than any cover girl he'd ever seen, and yet, despite all that, Desiree still said 'hi' to him in the hallways at school. She was Veronica's best friend, and that meant she knew Michael by proxy, and kinda-sorta had to be cordial to him when they bumped into each other at parties and whatever. But she was under no obligation to acknowledge his existence within the hallowed halls of Chelmsford High. And even if she was so obligated, she surely wasn't required to give him a smile on occasion, or a wave.

"...She's a lesbian, Michael," said Matt. "She might not know it yet, and Veronica is certainly too dim to notice, but Desiree is a certifiable rug-muncher."

"I don't believe you," said Michael. "The way she smiles at me. There's got to be something."

"Michael, she smiles at you because you blush the moment she makes eye contact. She's either getting some sort of perverted thrill out of watching you squirm in her presence, or she's just embarrassed."

"But you told me that she, back in the day, at the Roller Kingdom—"

"Yes, Michael. Back in the day, she was the handjob queen of the roller skating set. But she's not anymore. I think she fancies herself like some kind of second mother to that alien growing in my sister's abdomen. What you want, Michael, is—"

"I want Desiree," said Michael. "And you were supposed to be help—"

"You want the next Desiree, Michael. That's what you want."

"What do you mean?"

"Believe me, Michael. What you're in love with is not Desiree Emerson herself. What you're in love with is the very idea that a hot girl even knows you're alive. You're in love with the picture of her in the yearbook, the one that you jerk off to—"

"I do not!" said Michael, wondering how Matt could know. He had never done that down the Cape. And he had only done it half a dozen times here at home.

"Michael, please," said Matt. "I've been where you are now."

"Except you were jerking off to a picture of the football team."

Matt chuckled. "You got me there. But the difference isn't that big. What you're after, what you want now, is a quick physical fix. You don't need love. And you certainly don't need the bullshit baggage that comes with that word. You need a girl who's willing to rub your dick under the table at a roller skating rink while you sit back and eat French fries. I'm telling you, Michael. You should listen to me."

"And I suppose you know just the girl," said Michael.

"As a matter of fact," said Matt. "I do."

⚜

MICHAEL HAD NEVER BEEN on a date before, blind or otherwise, so he wasn't sure how this worked. Matt had made it sound so simple—'Just ask your dad for a ride to the Roller Kingdom,' he'd said. 'You think he's going to say no?'—but Michael knew it wouldn't be that easy. He could imagine the look on his father's face, that silly grin that Albert wore sometimes, and he didn't want to deal with that. He wanted an answer without any stupid questions—'A date, huh? With a girl?'—and without any embarrassing pats on the back, or on the shoulder. He didn't want Albert to be proud of him, to agree to drive him only after a thorough cross-examination. He wanted to present the facts of his situation all at once, and to receive a simple yes or a no, and then he wanted to be done with it. A couple of years from now, when he had a license of his own, this would be so simple— 'Dad, I'm going out.' 'Where?' 'Roller Kingdom.' 'Be back before eleven.'—and he saw no reason why it shouldn't be simple now.

So, Michael wrote a note. He wrote a note, explaining the whole situation, stuffed it into an envelope addressed to Mom & Dad (knowing full-well that Mom would never have the time to read it), and hung it on the refrigerator door with a magnet in the shape of Idaho, the only one of the fifty state magnets that had once adorned their fridge that Ashley hadn't yet stolen for use in her room.

God, Michael thought to himself, what if Ashley reads it? He looked at himself in the mirror he'd hung on the wall in front of his drafting table, and sure enough, he was the color of a boiling lobster, about to shuffle off to crustacean heaven.

There was a knock at the door.

"What?" said Michael.

"It's Dad," said Albert, from behind the door. "When do you want to leave?"

Michael closed his eyes and breathed in deep. "Six?" he said.

"Okay," said Albert. "Six it is."

Michael listened to his father's heavy footsteps descending the creaky staircase. Once he'd heard Albert reach the bottom, he leapt up onto his bed and did a little dance.

Now, he thought, if only I knew what to wear.

❧

ACCORDING TO MATT, Friday was metal night at the Roller Kingdom. And, seeing as Michael didn't listen to metal on a regular basis—Aerosmith was about the hardest rock he was into—there wasn't exactly a surplus of black t-shirts and leather jackets in his closet. No, his closet was full of comic book boxes—four long, two short—a bin of old Transformers and Star Wars figures, and just enough clothes to keep him from wearing the same thing at school twice in one week. The 'coolest' ensemble he owned, at least in is opinion, was a pair of faded blue jeans that were frayed at the cuffs, and a white tee emblazoned with the image of the comic book character Wolverine eviscerating two ninjas while in the midst of a berserker rage. That was about it, and because it was cold out, and he had no other choice, he wore his maroon and white Chelmsford jacket on top. Perhaps he could've pulled that off as cool if he'd actually lettered in something—in band, or in some non-jocky sport like track—but he wasn't sure. He calmed himself by repeating in his brain, 'I'll take it off the second I get in there. The very moment I get out of Dad's car even.'

But he was nervous about something else, too. Say this girl, this Marnie that Matt had set him up with, really did rub him underneath the table on the first date. Say that happened, and say he got all the way there, just from that. Would anyone be able to tell through his blue jeans? Is that why guys wore black jeans in the first place, to hide the evidence of the hand jobs they got? Should he have brought an extra pair of underwear, just in case? Yeah, maybe he should have. But then, where would he have stored them? His jacket didn't have an inside pocket, and he couldn't risk them falling out of an outside pocket onto the floor. Maybe he should have just worn one pair over the other.

"Michael," said Albert. "You look tense."

"Well," said Michael. "I, uh... I've never met this girl before."

"But Matt knows her, right? And he says she's alright."

"Well, she's his boyfriend's younger sister," said Michael. "Isn't he, like, obligated to say nice things about her."

Albert grinned, patted Michael on the shoulder. "I'm sure everything will be fine."

"And I've never skated before either," said Michael.

"Don't worry about that," said Albert. "Everyone looks like an ass on roller skates, even people who've been doing it for years."

"Thanks, Dad," said Michael, and he was thankful, thankful that a pat on the shoulder was all he got, that his father had stopped short of ruffling his hair.

❧

ALBERT DROPPED him off at a respectable distance from the front door, and told him to be back in the same spot by ten. Michael grunted his assent, gave Albert a wave, and began his long, lonely march toward the yellow glow of the front door. Underneath the awning, a guy in a jean jacket prodded a guy in a leather jacket and pointed toward Michael.

"Terry, lookit what we have here," said the guy in the jean jacket.

Terry chuckled. "It appears to be one of Chelmsford's finest, Brooks."

Michael let loose a heavy sigh, and ducked his head.

"Is that your boyfriend's jacket?" asked Brooks.

Michael pushed past him toward the door, ignoring the remark.

"It's got to be," said Terry, slapping a hand against the door, holding it closed. "Because the only sport this guy could letter in is—"

"It's the only jacket I own," said Michael, raising his gaze to meet theirs for the first time. "Okay? And it was a gift."

Terry moved his hand. "A gift from your boyfriend," he said.

Michael stormed inside, but he could hear their footsteps behind him. Brooks threw an arm around Michael's shoulders. "We're just fucking with you," he said with a laugh.

"Yeah," said Terry. "Unless you want us to, you know, fuck with you."

"In which case, we're going to have to refer you to our good friend Marnie over there by the snack bar."

"Marnie?" said Michael.

His two antagonists exchanged dumbfounded stares.

"What?" said Michael.

"You're the blind date?" said Terry.

"Matty Silver's cousin? Vern Silver's cousin?" said Brooks.

"You know my cousins?" said Michael.

"Why didn't you say something?" said Terry.

"We totally would have laid off," said Brooks.

"Well, you didn't give me much of a chance," said Michael, eyeing the giantess making her way across the room. "Is that?" asked Michael in a whisper.

"She only looks that tall from a distance," said Brooks.

"Yeah," said Terry. "Up close, she's like a veritable midget."

Marnie was tall and full-bodied. Not fat, just substantial. Michael imagined she was a basketball player on non-Metal nights, or a volleyball player. The arms that filled her tight leather coat were not the twigs Michael saw as he glanced around the rest of the room; they were thick branches. And though her body was imposing, the sheer size of her, the warm smiling face she presented to him from way up high was comforting enough to make up for it. Her round glasses softened her, as did the shoulder-length halo of golden hair that surrounded her smooth face.

"You're, like, the perfect height," said Marnie, with a wink.

"For what?" said Michael, not sure whether to stare directly at her breasts, which were at eye level, and which seemed to curve just the slightest bit upward, like an outstretched finger inviting him to come closer, to have a look, or if he was supposed to look up, toward her face, and do his best not to fixate on the insides of her nostrils.

Marnie laughed. "So innocent, too," she said.

Michael smiled. Brooks and Terry each gave him a slap on the back. Terry spoke first. "Well, Mister Silver, we're off. We've got to speak to the DJ about this black album bullshit he's pulling on us tonight."

"Yeah," Brooks groaned, as they walked away. "If you're gonna force Metallica down our throats, at least play something from *Puppets*, or *And Justice For All* even..."

Marnie took Michael's hand. Her grip was strong, perhaps a little too strong.

"C'mon," she said. "Buy me some fries and a drink, and I promise I'll make it worth your while."

Michael nodded his head, and let her lead him toward the snack bar, toward whatever came next.

"Stop laughing," Michael told Matt when he got him on the phone the next day, when it seemed like there was a hyena on the other end of the line instead of his cousin.

"Hey," said Matt, trying to catch his breath between chortles. "You got what you were after, didn't you?"

"She tugged at my dick like it was a fucking joystick," said Michael. "I'm afraid to even take a piss this morning because of how much it aches."

Matt kept on laughing. "I've always appreciated a firm grip," he said.

"Of course you have!" said Michael. "You're fucking gay!"

"She's the only girl who ever got me off," said Matt, who sounded like he was crying now.

Michael grunted, then hung up. He let himself fall backwards onto his bed and reached for the open yearbook on the floor. He gave Desiree one last look, then closed the book.

AL AND ROB

I n all the years he'd been drinking down the Legion, Albert Silver had never quite been able to shake the feeling that he didn't belong. He knew that the guys there loved him, loved him for his off-color jokes, for the way he kept a party going when he was spinning records, and, of course, for his ability to throw a nearly perfect game of Cricket when their darts team was in danger of losing bragging rights to some dive bar over in Lowell. He knew that they didn't hold it against him that the war had ended just a few weeks before his number came up, that he was as welcome here as anyone else with a paycheck to blow on a Friday night, vet or not. But he took little comfort in their acceptance of him. He remembered what he had said to his older brother when he went off to serve—"So long, babykiller!"—and, by extension, wasn't it what he had said to them all? If they knew what he had said, would they still be as understanding? Or would he be out on his ass?

Albert finished his Bud and set the bottle down. Across the table, his brother ashed the last of his Parliament Lights into the neck of his own empty bottle. Robert was the Silver that should have been the hero here at the bar. He was the one who had served with them,

who had done his duty. But Robert was also the sort of guy who saun-
tered into a working-class bar in a thousand-dollar suit, the sort of
guy who drove a Jag into parking lot full of Fords and Chevys, the
sort of guy who, when you asked for a light, handed you a matchbook
inscribed with his self-proclaimed title, "Auto King of New England."

"You want something else to drink?" asked Albert.

"I'm all set," said Robert. And of course he was all set, because
he was a somebody in this town. And somebodies didn't get
wasted in public. After all, they couldn't afford to lose their cool
in front of potential customers. No, they only got shitfaced at
home, where the recipients of their tirades, of their slaps and
their insults, would keep things quiet.

Robert crushed the last of his cigarette into the tray, then
rubbed his hands together as if trying to shake off a chill. He
asked, "You heard about Veronica?"

Albert nodded. He had heard. From his daughter Ashley, of all
people, who didn't even go to the high school yet, whose class-
mates used the gossip that their older siblings brought home as
further ammunition in their seemingly constant war against her. 'I
hear sluttiness runs in families,' one girl was supposed to have
said, 'and seeing as you're never going to get a boyfriend with your
looks, you should consider yourself lucky.'

"I'm thinking of putting my foot down," said Robert.

"How so?"

"Gonna force them to do it right, if I have to. The kid seems
like he's willing to do the right thing. It's Veronica who's giving
me trouble."

"Well, she's only seventeen, Rob. What do you expect?"

"I expected her to know better than to get herself into the
same situation her mother and me got ourselves into. I expected
her to have learned from her brother's mistakes and realized
where this kind of life gets you." Robert paused. "Well, all I gotta
say is: she may not have lived up to expectations before, but she

damn well better live up to expectations now if she expects one bit of support from me."

"Lyd feel the same way?" asked Albert.

"I don't care how Lyd feels, or what Lyd thinks. She hasn't lived up to expectations neither. You think she ever really tried to instill in our daughter what could happen to her if she screwed up? You think Lyd ever *really* tried?"

No, Albert thought. Lydia had probably never tried instilling any such thing in her daughter. Because, the truth was, Lydia didn't see things the way that Robert did. She didn't look back at the evening that resulted in her son as a mistake, even if she hadn't exactly wanted to be at that party, or in that bedroom, or with this man. And she didn't view the surprise arrival of her daughter some five years later as an accident, although they hadn't planned for her, and had, in fact, been planning for some time apart. Lydia, in her own quiet way, was every bit the good Christian that Robert loudly proclaimed himself to be. She had faith in God's guiding light, in His grand design. She saw blessings where Robert saw curses.

"This ain't the sort of thing you usually bring up in public," said Albert.

"Well, I wanted to talk about my options without someone blowing up in my face. I figured you'd keep it down, that you wouldn't want to make a scene."

Albert shook his head. "I wouldn't have made a scene in private either, Rob."

Robert nodded. "Yeah, I suppose you wouldn't have."

"You don't tell me how to raise my kids, and I don't tell you how to raise yours," said Albert. "That's always been our agreement, right?"

"Sure," said Robert, taking a drag.

"You gonna kick her out if she says no?" asked Albert.

Robert nodded slowly, letting the smoke spill out from his

nostrils. "Gotta give kids ultimatums. They don't understand much else."

"Where do you think she'll go, if you kick her out?"

Robert shook two fingers at Al, the stub of his cigarette clutched between them. "I thought you weren't going to tell me how to raise my—"

"Don't get bent out of shape here. I'm not telling you anything, Rob. I'm asking you something."

"Yeah, well, you got a way of asking things," said Robert. "Makes it sound like you're passing judgment."

"I'm not—"

"This is about Matt, ain't it?"

"Simmer down. You're getting a bit loud. Remember, everyone you meet is a potential—"

"Don't give me that shit!" Robert spat. "You think I shoulda given him a second chance? You think I shoulda brought him back into my home, that godless, ungrateful little faggot? I kicked him out outta love, Al. Outta love!"

"Yeah, Rob, I sensed a lot of fucking love in the room when you were trying to kill him with your bare fucking hands."

"Tough love, Al! You gotta be tough with your kids. Tough love!" he chanted. "You think Michael's ever gonna stop with the friggin' painting and do something serious with his life if you don't put some pressure on? You think Ashley's ever going to lose weight if you keep going easy on her?"

Albert stood up, his chair toppling backwards behind him. "Don't start with me on Ashley, Rob. Don't you fucking start."

The bartender called over, "You guys maybe wanna take this outside?"

"Nah," said Robert, heading for the door. "I'm leaving. We're done."

Albert called after his brother, "Hey, Auto King!"

Robert stopped at the door, and turned around again.

"Don't forget your lighter," said Albert, tossing him his ridiculous monogrammed Zippo.

"Thanks, asshole," said Robert.

"See you Easter?" asked Albert.

"See you Easter."

SITTING in his rumbling Ford Escort in front of old Phil Gates' place an hour or so later, waiting for Ashley to finish up her visit with Phil's kids Robin and Adam, Albert got to thinking, once again, about what Robert had said about 'tough love.' Where in the hell had he gotten that from? Albert recalled their parents' love as anything but tough. He supposed it could have been different for Rob, seeing as Rob was born first, but it couldn't have been that different, could it? Albert had been around to witness firsthand nearly all of Rob's spectacular childhood fuck-ups, from the time he cracked up the family car during a cross-town joyride at the age of twelve, to his first weekend bender during freshman year of high school, and never once did their parents react with 'tough love.' If anything, the love of Eli and Edna Silver was gentle to a fault. There was never any screaming, hardly ever so much as a raised voice. Punishments were more apt to consist of long, drawn-out discussions about the repercussions of their actions. They still got the old standards—'When I was your age' and, of course, 'Back in my day'—but that was about it. They had never been grounded, or sent to their room without supper, or forced into extra chores to make up for their transgressions. And Eli still had the same way about him to this day, that cool, measured demeanor that his grandchildren took advantage of every summer they spent down the Cape. The truth was that you were never going to get into much trouble with Eli Silver. He didn't police you; he expected you to police yourself. He thought that kind of responsibility was good for a kid, that it built character. Tough love—well, that didn't come from Eli Silver, that was for damn sure.

In his heart, Albert knew the truth. Robert disapproved of the way their parents had raised them. Rob believed that he had turned out well, *in spite of* their parents, and not because of them. He would never say so out loud—that wouldn't be the Christian thing to do—but he had been thinking it for years, even if he did bring a new vehicle down the Cape every couple of years as "repayment" for their tolerance of his misspent youth. The cars, the smiles, the deferring to Eli during the summers (at least until the summer of the Great Schism)—those were all for show. For a guy who disapproved of the arts as a career, who thought of them as a soft option, Robert's ability to play a role was astounding, Oscar-worthy even.

The Gates' dog yelped from behind their chain-link fence as Ashley made her way down the front steps, her face sullen, her shoulders slouched. She opened the passenger's side door and plopped herself down into the seat. Phil came to the door and waved as Ashley got herself settled. Albert waved back to his old classmate, and then they were off.

Ashley waited until they'd reached the end of Quigley, until Albert had turned on his directional to turn left onto Middlesex, before she lit into him. "Why did you have to pick me up? Why couldn't I have stayed? We were gonna beat that game! What's there to do at home? Why couldn't I have slept over?"

"First of all," Albert interjected, "it supposed to snow like a bastard tonight and tomorrow, and I want you under our roof and not halfway across town when the storm hits."

"Fine," said Ashley. "Whatever."

"And secondly, I think you're a little young to be staying over a boy's house."

"It's Robin's house, too," said Ashley. "I'm friends with her, too."

"I understand that," said Albert.

"But you think I'm going to turn out like Veronica."

Albert glanced over at his daughter. He wasn't sure what to say. The truth was that he was afraid of his baby getting pregnant, as he imagined every father of every girl in the whole world must be. He knew that they'd deal with it if it happened, that they'd get through it, that he wouldn't be throwing her out of his house no matter what. But that didn't make thinking about it any easier. She was just barely old enough for it to be a rational fear—to the best of his knowledge, she'd gotten her period for the first time just last month—but it was a fear of his nevertheless. Sure, it was possible that her relationship with Adam was entirely chaste. And there was the older sibling there to consider too, the third wheel that would keep the pair of them from taking off to places they weren't ready to go, but the boy was thirteen. And thirteen year old boys, if he recalled correctly, were a determined lot, obsessed, for the most part, with only one thing. That one thing that consistently got both boys and girls in trouble, and lots of it.

"...as if any boy would even think about fooling around with me," Ashley was saying. "They wouldn't even think about it, let alone try something."

"You're too hard on yourself, Ash." And she really was. Because, yes, she may have been heavy. She may have even been what her doctor called her: obese. But the weight was only temporary. She still had her mother's face, that flawless, undistilled, Scandinavian face. And while it wouldn't launch a thousand ships anytime soon, especially not with the amount of time it spent clenched in a scowl, Albert was sure that, with a little work, it might one day.

"Whatever," she said, sulking.

"You don't think there's any boy out there who's thought about—"

"You're drunk," said Ashley.

Albert sighed. He wasn't drunk. Ashley *knew* he wasn't drunk. But this was her way of ending a conversation. It was one of her favorite tactics. She knew he was sensitive about how much he drank, about whether or not that constituted too much, and she played him like a fiddle.

"I'm not drunk," Albert told her.

"You're totally drunk," said Ashley. "I can smell it on you. You shouldn't even be driving. Pull over," she said. "I'll drive."

"Ashley, you're twelve—"

"Yeah," she said, taking a new tack, "and that means my dad totally shouldn't be talking to me about boys. If anyone should be talking to me about boys, it should be Mom." She paused for a moment, and then added hastily, "And I don't want her to talk to me about boys either."

"OK," said Albert. "Fine."

"We were so close," she said. "Adam's probably on the final boss right now."

"I'm sorry to take you away from your game," said Albert. "Your mother and I will just feel a lot safer with you home with us during the storm."

"OK," said Ashley. "I get it."

"I'm not trying to ruin your day, Ash. I'm just—"

"You're drunk," said Ashley, smirking.

Albert smirked himself, then nodded.

"What about Mom?".

"She might be stuck at the hospital for a little while," said Albert. "But the hospital's safe, too," he added, as an afterthought.

Ashley bit her lower lip and nodded. "Can I turn on the radio?" she asked.

Albert nodded in reply, Ashley turned on the radio, and for the rest of the ride home they just listened.

LATE THAT NIGHT, standing on the porch with the cordless phone to his ear, half-listening to his wife relaying the details of her day—"two sections in the morning... a breach in the afternoon"—Albert marveled at the April snow. This was one of the things he loved the most about life in New England, the sheer unpredictability of it. Snow in April was not unheard of—hell, he was pretty sure it had snowed here in June, once upon a time—but snow like this, driving snow that just wouldn't quit... well, that was a whole other thing. You could never tell when something like this was going to happen. This was *life*. Whatever will be will be, and all that jazz. If God had a plan, and Albert wasn't even sure if there was a God out there to make plans, then the plan was this: let's see what happens.

Robert could never understand that, Robert, who wanted people to live up to expectations, who wanted everything to go according the agenda he laid out on his desk calendar each and every day. Robert hated the winter in general, and snowstorms in particular. "Bad for business," he would say. And sure, they were—who wanted to buy a car buried under a foot of snow, after all?—but his real point was that anything unpredictable would be better off done away with. There was a scene in the second *Back to the Future* movie which Robert constantly referred to when it came to the weather. In the future, the movie suggested, there would be a weather service that regulated all forms of precipitation. And that day, Robert said, couldn't come soon enough.

If he were Veronica's father, Albert liked to think that this whole ordeal wouldn't be an ordeal at all. Sure, the pregnancy was unexpected. But Veronica was seventeen, she was graduating from high school in a couple of months, and the father of the baby was willing to do his share. Veronica hadn't run off to get herself an abortion; she'd thought long and hard about things instead. The situation, Albert thought, had worked out about as well as it could have.

"So, how was your day?" Michaela asked him.

"Fine," said Albert. "Met up with Rob down the Legion. Talked about Veronica, among other things."

"And how'd that go?"

Albert grunted.

"That well?"

"The kids are getting older, Mikki. Robert doesn't want to accept it. Hell, I'm not even sure I want to accept it. But the fact is that they're getting older faster than we're getting ready for them to be older." Albert paused, not sure what he was driving at. "Promise me, Mik, that no matter what kind of trouble our kids get themselves into, that we'll always be there for them."

"Of course," said Michaela.

"And that we won't use threats and ultimatums to make them do what we want them to do, that we'll let them be who they want to—"

"What's Rob threatening Veronica with?"

"Just promise me," he said.

"I promise," said Michaela.

"You looked outside lately?" he asked her, keen to change the subject, to move on.

"It's snowing," she said.

"Like a bastard," he said. "It's amazing to watch. So damn random."

"Al," she said. "Are you drunk?"

Albert laughed. "No, Mik, I'm not drunk." He watched the snow fly across the narrow beam of the lamplight, so fast, so determined. Silver streaking across gold. "I'm stone-cold sober," he told his wife. "Stone-cold sober."

ROBIN

THE WORD ON THE CEILING

The last time I saw David alive, he said something to me that made me want to kill him. I didn't kill him, of course. But, oh, the murderous thoughts of a jaded teenage girl. When you're young, and nubile, and death is like some story your grandparents tell, like walking uphill to school both ways in the driving snow, or like glass bottles of fresh milk waiting on the doorstep by the dawn's early light—well then, when death is something like that, something that will never happen to you, then you'll wish it upon anyone, won't you? For even the most innocent trespass.

Ah, trespasses. *Forgive us our trespasses as we forgive those who trespass against us.* My father's words ring in my ears, and I remember him kneeling by my bedside until I got it right, until I did it without the lisp. Me in my white nightdress, my naked arms beet-red with shame, and he in his flannel pajamas, reeking wonderfully of clove cigarettes. Oh, his valiant effort to stamp out my sibilant S! Daddy, if you were here today, you would see it in my eyes—I tried to forgive him; I really did. But you didn't see the way he looked at me when he said it, like some kind of scavenger, hoarding away the pieces of me that would be useful for a song, or a poem, and casting aside the rest of me like so much gristle.

"You know, you guys are turning into John and Yoko," he hissed at me as I hoisted my amp into the trunk of my car.

"That's not fair," I said, turning to face him, scowling, "I helped you start this band."

"I know," he said, wiping sweat from his brow, squinting in the July sun. "You're John. *He's* Yoko."

He stalked off, rounding the corner of the chain-link fence that surrounded his house, slipping in through the side gate, and then latching it behind himself.

"I QUIT!" I shouted. But he didn't look back. David, for all his histrionics regarding the ascension of Michael and me to the forefront of the band, was still our leader, our conductor. And he had orchestrated this whole scene. He didn't need to look back at me. He didn't need to listen. He wouldn't need to listen later that night either, when Michael called him to scream his own resignation and to end their lifelong friendship with a litany of four letter words. The codas of David Johnson's compositions never strayed far from the notes on the page.

For a time, it had been an admirable quality, David's mastery over the situation at hand. I can recall, with misty eyes, that night, all those years ago, when David massaged my shoulders in the darkened hallway behind our school's auditorium. Behind us, on stage, the orchestra was running through the theme from *Schindler's List*. My ex-boyfriend—that dreaded prefix a wound still fresh—was the first-chair violin, and I was listening intently to each of his solos, waiting for him to hit that one bad note that would give me some sense of closure, speaking aloud, "Damn," at the end of each line he ran through without flaw.

Around us, other kids milled about, also waiting to return to the stage, speaking in breathy whispers to one another. I closed my eyes as David's fingers worked at the knots in my neck. He asked me how it felt and all I could manage was a heavy sigh.

"Robin," David said to me, as his fingers kneaded down my back, "you need to calm down. He's not going to screw up. I mean, for every knot I get out, two more pop up in its place."

"I'm sorry," I said.

"Don't be sorry," he said, finding a spot in my lower back more twisted up than anything he'd already worked on. "Just be happy."

I let out a loud, low moan—almost guttural—that I hadn't expected. People in the crowd that wandered about us stopped their own conversations and stared at me, at us, but I didn't care. I didn't care, couldn't care, about anything in the world. David had found that part of me that no boyfriend had ever dared to venture near. But he was unafraid. He knew what must be done, and he did it. It was the way of his life—he went for what he wanted. With one notable exception, of course, and that was me.

The rumor mill at our high school, like the great mills of the last century, whose hulking brick husks still dotted the banks of the nearby Merrimack River, cast the shadow of an overbearing juggernaut over the student body. Run at the top by rich, untouchable WASPs, it was efficient and often deadly (at least to the reputation) for those who lingered too close to the machinery of the thing. And David was one of its favorite victims.

Thin of frame and pale as Stoker's Transylvanian Count, David was cursed with all of the features that the real vampires of our world—the social vampires, that is—craved in their victims. Soft-spoken, with a quasi-falsetto, and a sibilant S his own father hadn't cared to correct, he was also possessed of the limp wrists and bitchy demeanor of the omnipresent queenish caricature that dominated our popular culture. And the girls like me, who clung to him in the hallways, offered no proof of innocence. No, we were fag-hags, a word often found on the lips of cheerleaders and preppy girls, but one never spoken aloud.

It was because of this rumor mill and because of the fact that some of our friends and acquaintances had actually begun to believe it, that David could never bring himself to approach me in the way that a friend of his soon would.

"I'm not dating any more musicians," I promised him, as we filed onto the stage that night for our own performance, me with my clarinet and he with his sax. And all that he could muster, when most boys in his position would have at least made some pronouncement that not all musicians were bad, that he, at the very least, was not like that—all that he could muster was a smirk across his bright pouty lips, a pat on my shoulder, and the words, "Yes, maybe that's for the best."

It was around then that David and I had decided to start a band of our own. "The Smashing Pumpkins on woodwinds?" I had teased him, before he clarified his intentions for he and I to play rhythm and lead guitar respectively. A portly friend of his from Scout camp, Billy Mills, would play the drums. And there was a bass-playing biker who hung out at the comic book store where David worked, a guy who'd been telling David for months to name the time and place for a jam. We were all set with our little four-piece. David and I would take turns singing. It was going to be brilliant. And then came a most unexpected development.

I REMEMBER the night I met Michael Silver so well that it hurts. Wind was whipping against the windows of David's mom's house, rattling them. And it was cold outside, too cold for anything but a force of nature to be moving about. But traffic persisted nevertheless, horns honking, breaks squealing, cars skidding on the black ice and struggling to regain control. David and I sat in the comfort of his living room, the heat cranked up, and we strummed the chords to R.E.M.'s "Man on the Moon"—me on lead, David on rhythm—trying to recapture the right combination of country twang and alternative strangeness from the original recording.

I sang, "Let's play Twister. Let's play risk."

David added, "Yeah, yeah. Yeah, yeah."

"I'll see you in heaven if you make the list."

"Yeah, yeah. Yeah, yeah."

The one part I couldn't get, no matter how hard I tried, was the little bit were Stipe channels Elvis Presley on the vocals. First you sing, normally, "Now Andy, are you goofin' on Elvis?" and then you're supposed to imitate Elvis: "Hey baby!" and then quickly go back to normal with, "Are we losing touch?" I could never quite get the "Hey baby!" and I caught one of David's grins out of the corner of my eye each time I tried.

His house always smelled funny. David's mom never cooked for her son, but for their dog, a pitch-black ball of fat and fur that barked at walls, she would warm exotically spiced bones that stunk up the whole place. David was cooking French fries and fish sticks in that same oven now. He'd offered me some, but I had politely declined. Something about cooking human food in the same oven that you heated dog bones in—something about that didn't sit well with me.

The oven timer went off and, while I finished playing "Man on the Moon," David put his guitar aside and headed for the kitchen. As I worked through the last refrain, he returned, his food on a paper plate. He sat on the floor, by the coffee table, and sprinkled the fish and fries with liberal amounts of salt and pepper. When I was through with the song, he clapped, and once he'd chewed away the mouthful of food that filled his maw, he proceeded with the compliments.

"As ever, that was amazing," he said. "I hope my playing didn't screw you up."

"You were fine," I assured him. "You always do fine. You shouldn't be so hard on yourself."

He blushed. "Well," he said, "I appreciate that. I know you're lying, but I appreciate the deceit."

I smiled at him as I set my guitar back in its hard plastic case. "When's your friend supposed to get here?"

David rubbed the grease off of his hands onto a paper towel. He reached inside his jacket and pulled out his gold pocket watch, something we'd picked up on a trip together into Boston. I remembered all the trouble he'd gone through to get us there. I was still two to three months shy of getting my license, and he was a full year from getting his. We'd had to have his grandparents drive us to the train station in Lowell, cramped into a backseat already full with an archaic baby seat that hadn't been used since David was a child. It was at the Faneuil Hall marketplace that we found the watch. After stuffing ourselves on samples from the eateries that lined the main hall—a piece of pizza here, some chowder there, a cookie from the Boston Chipyard to finish us off —we found ourselves meandering past the little carts in the glass-enclosed side hall. And that's when we spotted it. The watch looked more expensive than it was, of course, but even that was too expensive for two high school kids. David always had money on him, though. There seemed to be a silent agreement between him and his mother—she could neglect him completely and totally, so long as she understood and did not complain when he rifled through her purse for his per diem. And so, that was that. He bought the watch.

David flipped it open, flipped it closed again, and then put it away. "He should be here any minute," he said. But he looked nervous. There was a concert to go to that night, and his friend was our ride. David stood, picked up his plate, and ate while he paced.

"Do I look alright?" he asked.

I gave him a once-over and, finding his outfit, on the whole, to be standard-issue slacker—blue jeans, concert tee, red and white Chucks—I gave him a nod. "But what's with the smoking jacket?"

He shrugged. "You don't think it goes?"

I shook my head. "Nah, man. It goes. It just... maybe it doesn't go to a Nine Inch Nails show."

He stopped in his tracks and set his plate down on the arm of the couch, stalking off toward the bathroom.

I looked down at his plate and saw something amiss. "There's no ketchup," I pointed out.

"Ketchup is unnatural," he said, coming back, taking off the jacket. "Tomatoes in a bottle? Does that seem right to you?"

I don't think I would've been able to eat what he was eating without drenching it in some condiment, but I nodded along as if I understood.

Suddenly, there were four quick knocks upon the heavy wooden door. The dog began to yelp with all of the might that it could muster in its tiny little lungs, and the pooch's outburst was the straw that broke poor David's back. He huffed as he stood to get the door. "I don't understand why he doesn't just come in. I've told him a thousand times."

While his back was to me, I reached across the table to pluck a fry from his plate. It was so soggy and disgusting that I might not have finished it if it weren't for the fact that I had no place to hide the evidence. I chewed quickly, swallowed, and reached for my Diet Coke.

At the door, David groaned, saying to the as-yet-unseen friend, "I don't understand why you don't just come in."

The boy shrugged as he followed David into the living room. Though I was sure I had seen him in the halls once or twice, I had never gotten a really good look at Mister Michael Silver until that afternoon. I stood to greet him and shook his hand.

He was the best kind of handsome: the kind that doesn't know it yet and maybe never will. His longish brown hair was unkempt, and he had missed a spot shaving just under his chin, but he had haunting hazel eyes and a wide smile to make up for it. He could've used a little help dressing himself—there were paint stains here and there on his jeans and a small tear near the bottom of his faded t-shirt—but that was part of the charm.

I tugged at the tiny padlock that hung from my chain-link choker. "We've met before, haven't we?"

David nodded. "He used to play AD&D with Adam and Ashley and me, down at the comic book store. You might have seen him there."

"Wait," I said, in recognition of his sister's name. "Ashley Silver?"

"That's my sister," said Michael.

Without really knowing why I was doing it, I slapped him on the shoulder. "I didn't even know she had a brother. When she comes over to visit my brother, she never says a thing about you."

"Well," said Michael, "my parents have always told her that if she doesn't have anything nice to say about someone, she shouldn't say anything at all."

I laughed, and for the second time in as many minutes I made some absurd gesture to get closer to him, bumping my hip into his side. "What could she possibly have to say about you that's so bad?"

David clicked his pocket watch open, then shut it again, and right then, right then I should've known that it was all going to go to hell. You know those moments? That was one of those moments, the clicking shut of the watch like the closing of a door. "Time to go," said David.

I slipped on my pea coat and picked up my guitar case, holding it up for Michael to see. "Could you drop me off after?"

He nodded and smiled. "Absolutely," he said, as we headed outside, to the car.

"So, you play guitar?" Michael asked me.

David groaned.

"Yeah. You play?" I asked.

"No. I sing," said Michael, unlocking and opening the rear door for me. "A little," he added hastily.

I slid my guitar case into the backseat and, not yet ready to exchange his face for the back of his head, I rubbed his shoulder and said, "David and I are thinking of starting a band. You should be our singer."

"Maybe," said Michael, smiling. He turned to see what David thought, as did I, but David had already gotten into the passenger's seat and turned up the radio. Michael nodded at me and said, "That might be fun."

❧

MICHAEL DROVE A GRAY FORD TEMPO, a four-door sedan that was falling apart in every way imaginable. There were lights illuminated on the dash that shouldn't have been lit, and noises coming from places that should have been silent, but once we hit the road, and the music was going, we forgot about the problems. David manned the stereo, inserting tapes when necessary, fast-forwarding as needed. We all sang along.

And Michael could sing. He could really sing. His voice was heavy, and warm, and untrained, and when he hit a note he didn't hit it because it was what he was taught to do. He hit that note because it felt right, because it felt good. He had a real man's voice when he sang. It was sure, and true.

It was, honestly, the sexiest voice I'd ever heard.

I didn't know where he came from though, because he wasn't in band or chorus or even the theatre guild. He had never been seen in our hallway at the high school, had never even skirted the edges of our clique. I, like so many of my friends at the time, thought that I knew everyone in our school who had any musical talent whatsoever. Never in my life had I been more happy to be wrong.

To hear him sing, to hit the notes without even seeming to think about them, to get the emotion right—he had me. I wanted to know this guy. I wanted to be around him. And it was during the concert that I made my move.

❧

I<small>T WAS</small> few songs in when people began to leap over our heads. I watched one sweaty goth boy after another plummet down to the concrete floor below, each of them landing, like a cat, on their feet, then rushing past distracted security guards into the fray of the mosh pit. The security guards were trying to turn back the tide of young bodies driving, like a wedge, down from the upper level of the stadium, toward the floor. For a moment, when the march down the metal stairs had begun, I was shooting glances over at Michael, sort of a silent question: You want to try it? But he had looked over at David, who appeared petrified by the whole ordeal, and he had shaken his head with a small frown.

It didn't help the situation that, over the driving drumbeat, the singer was goading the crowd, "Step right up! March! Push! Crawl right up on your knees!"

In front of us, the railings on either side of the steel staircase began to buckle. Lights flashed out across the audience as the music disappeared, save a simple piano line, and the singer's pleading question, "Now, doesn't it make you feel better?" Thousands of bodies writhed in time to the music as the lights went down again, the drumbeat heavy, driving, like an oncoming train.

I couldn't help but stare at Michael as he sang along. He knew all the words. His face—contorted, crunched up, locked in a perpetual scream—seemed to betray a true understanding of each lyric. David sat in his corner, staring ahead at the stage, listening intently, but I could not sit back and let the music simply wash over me, as my friend was doing. I saw Michael and it was like he was part of the music, so when the opportunity presented itself, I sang with him, to him.

We screamed together, "Devils speak of the way in which

she'll manifest," and Michael leaned back, as if the thick, slow crunch of the guitar was actually a physical force bending his body. "Angels bleed from the tainted touch of my caress," we sang, our voices just two amongst a chorus of thousands. "Need to contaminate, to alleviate, this loneliness!" we sang, eyes forward, toward the stage. And then I grabbed hold of him by the shoulders and we sang to each other, "I now know the depths I reach are limitless."

Years later, upon learning of my indiscretions with redheaded jazz drummer I'd met while studying at Berklee, Michael would quote from the same song in an email written to break off our relationship. Older, and perhaps a little wiser, he would still be compelled to use the vocabulary of our youth. The time would come when all I was to him was the beautiful liar, the precious whore of this bitter, vengeful song. And perhaps I should have known, with the way that we started, that I would never be the girl in the white dress for him, standing by the ocean, proclaiming my love as tears trickled down over the precipice of my fat lashes. Perhaps I should have known that I was not that girl, that that girl was still to come for him. And knowing that, perhaps I shouldn't have done what I did the night of the concert. Perhaps I shouldn't have thrown away what I already had.

Perhaps, perhaps, perhaps! If two roads diverged in a wood that I was traveling through, isn't it apparent now, so sickeningly apparent, which one would I choose?

I stood with Michael outside the men's room after that show, waiting for David. My overworked ear drums throbbed with a dull, familiar ache, while I watched this boy, more limited in his concert-going experience, rub at his Adam's apple. His hair was matted with sweat, his t-shirt clinging to his soft, unthreatening frame as he hunched over to catch his breath.

"Good show, huh?" I asked him.

He nodded and smiled, looking at me only briefly before

casting his eyes back down upon the floor, determined not to play Judas. If only both of us had been so determined.

"They play everything you wanted to hear?" I asked.

"I was hoping they'd do 'Heresy.' It's become my, sort-of... I don't know... my anthem."

I grinned. "God is dead, huh?"

"I don't even know if that's what he's saying in the song, though. I think it's more about why God sucks. You know, 'he flexed his muscles, to keep his flock of sheep in line. He made a virus, that would kill off all the swine.' And, of course, you know, the 'perfect kingdom of suffering and pain' part... I don't think he really believes God is dead. I think he's just saying that to piss God off."

I nodded along. "I get it," I said, drawing closer. "You're really into it. I like that."

"My grandfather passed away last spring," he said, his voice soft and raspy, barely audible above the din of the departing crowds. "I guess that's when I started to connect with all the lyrics, all the words about loss and anger and stuff." He paused and rubbed his throat again, coughing a little.

I leaned toward him, tilting my head, and pressed my lips against the spot where he'd been rubbing. His stubble prickled against my face and sent shivers down to the tips of my toes. I wanted to wrap myself up in him and it was with great reluctance that I pulled away, rubbing a hand along his arm, asking him, "All better?"

His eyes were open, but they weren't on me. From behind us I heard the voice I had begun to dread. Donning a deeper, more masculine tone, unashamed of the artifice of it all, David asked Michael, "Can we go? Robin and I both have a French test tomorrow."

Michael nodded. "Sorry," he said. "I didn't know."

FOR A WHILE, the tension worked. Like Fleetwood Mac, whose song "Go Your Own Way" would become one of our band's staples, we fed off of the discontent. Too dignified to have out-and-out rows with each other in normal conversation, we left our most bitter barbs for our songs where, supposedly veiled, we were supposed to judge them only on their merit as songs. And it wasn't as hard as you'd imagine. When Michael and I sang harmonies on David's "A Toast to the Duplicitous," with it's nods to The Cars' 'Best Friend's Girl' and the Beatles 'Rocky Raccoon,' the composition was so strong, the vocals so warm and lush, that it was easy to become lost in the music, to forget that Michael was the rival whose legs were to be shot off.

Yes, for a while it worked. For a while, David held himself back. He glared at us—oh, how he glared—and he made snide remarks under his breath, but the music was something special. He knew what we were doing was quite beyond high school standards, that if he gave it time he could parlay it into future success. But the puppeteer will only suffer the willful insubordination of his marionettes for so long. David was no Geppetto. Sing to him of your newfound freedom—I've got no strings, and so on—and you would not be likely to find a smile upon his face.

On the eve of our band's dissolution, we were to be found, as was so often the case in our misspent youth, within the confines of Michael's Ford Tempo. We sat in our usual configuration, David up front and me in the back—an inconvenient arrangement we had thus far conceded to David in an attempt to keep the peace. Despite his complaints of a headache, David had cranked the stereo. And I was doing my best not to groan at the playlist he'd prepared for us: a healthy dose of the mopiest Cure and Smiths songs he could find.

A couple of miles down the road from the Friendly's where we'd stopped for dinner, I started pushing my knee into the back of Michael's seat. And when that didn't get his attention, I started kicking it, losing my shoes in the process. The music was loud enough to mask the sound of my attack but, finally, not the feel of it. With his right hand on the wheel, Michael reached his left hand back through the crevice between the door and his seat and grabbed for my foot.

I kicked his hand away. When he relented, I pushed my knees into the back of his seat again. The second time he reached his hand back I let him grab hold of my ankle. David continued to sing along with the music but Michael had fallen silent. He held my foot and I felt his hand grow warm. With my other foot, I rubbed the top of his hand.

When we reached the Drum Hill rotary I thought to let him go, but he held on even tighter. With only his right hand on the wheel, he navigated the circular stretch of road. He missed our turn-off and kept going. David kept singing.

We were headed toward my house when the tape that was playing finished. As David fished around the front seat for another, I said, "I'm not ready to go home yet."

"Well, I, uhm, I'm tired," said David.

"Then we can drop you off first," I suggested. "I know that's breaking tradition and all, but... Michael, would you mind dropping David off first?"

"No. I, uh... Do you mind?" he asked David.

"No. Sure. It's fine."

When we reached his house, David got out of the car without a word to us and began his way up the stairs. I unbuckled my seatbelt and walked round the back of the car.

David turned and said to me, "He's flighty, you know. Can't keep focused on any one thing for too long. He left painting behind for the band. What's to say—"

I cut him off. "And what does that have to do with he and I?"

David smirked. "When he's off at college, what makes you think he's faithful?"

"He's a good guy, David."

He shivered in the unseasonable cold, pulling his smoking

jacket tighter around himself, unaware, even now, of how he would be wishing for just a moment of this chill the next day, when the warm front came through. "Yeah, he's a good guy. And you're a good girl, too. Faithful friends, the both of you." He grunted, stepping in through his front door. "Have fun parking, or whatever it is you call what you two do."

☙❧

IN HINDSIGHT, I would've pulled out of practice the next day. I should have. With things as hot as they were, nothing good ever could have come of it. But I went anyway, because I was convinced that we could make it through it, that we had to.

And in hindsight I'm sure that David, upon reading that head-line ten years hence, confirming that I had, in fact, met an end fitting of the man he'd once compared me to—I'm sure that even David would feel a tinge of regret for the words he'd uttered in haste. I'm sure that when he saw the headline—*Local singer shot dead*—that he too would have wished for a chance to do it all over again.

As the story goes, John Lennon met Yoko Ono on a visit to an exhibition of hers in London in 1966. Taken with the aesthetic and interactive nature of her work, which included a decomposing apple and an instruction to hammer a nail into a chunk of wood, Lennon's most famous anecdote regarding the exhibit related his experience of climbing a ladder to find the word 'Yes' written on the ceiling. In later interviews, he said that it was this one word that gave him cause to continue. If it had been 'No' written up there, he claimed, he would have walked straight out. But since it was 'Yes', since the message was one of positivity and, to his mind, possibility, he stayed; he continued on.

If I really were John, and Michael were Yoko, then I found myself wondering what word Michael would have written on the ceiling. And the thing is, I don't think it would have been yes, and

I don't think it would have been no. I'm almost certain that it would have been maybe, because yes and no are black and white. They're absolutes, and as David was apt to point out, given even the smallest occasion to do so, Michael was unaware of absolutes. He lacked dedication, commitment, and focus. But maybe, that most entropic of words—Michael's word—is where possibility truly lies.

AFTER THE PROM

I t wasn't the noise of them fucking that was keeping Matt awake; it was his own Goddamned erection. With a pillow over his head, he could escape the rhythmic creak of the old floorboards, the piercing squeaks of the poorly-assembled brass bed, and the shrill yelps of Michael's saucy little minx. But, pillow or no, he couldn't ignore Wee Willie Winkie standing at attention, eager to be recognized, unwilling to stand down.

A Monty Python tune hummed through his aching brain. *It's swell to have a stiffy; it's divine to own a dick.* "From the tiniest little tadger," he sang, under his breath. "To the world's biggest prick."

Maybe it was divine to own a dick, to have the choice to fill or be filled without the need for strapped-on attachments. But was it really swell to have a stiffy? Having a penis—well, that was something he'd always enjoyed. But the stiffy part, Mr. Happy's annoying habit of seeking attention at the worst possible times— baseball games, family dinners, those few mortifying minutes during confirmation—that, he could do without. He'd like to have a cock which responded only to the whims of, say, a remote control. Something small and thin that he could carry in his back pocket. A pause button for those drunken evenings when holding the piss back even one more moment seemed impossible. Rewind for those nights when a guy was hitting the spot too hard and too fast, fast-forward for those twilit trysts which were never over soon enough. A simple on-off switch to keep him out of trouble. And when he found the right guy, he would hand the device over, as a token of his love and affection. It would be a much more practical gift than a gold ring.

Unless, of course, it was a gold cock-ring. That would be... well, that would be...

Matt held the pillow tighter over his own head, hoping to drown out the sound of his own thoughts as well as he was drowning out the sound of his teenaged cousin's post-prom humpfest. A gold cock-ring?!? He was full of shit, and he fucking knew it. He'd never even seen a cock-ring. And, aside from his own, he hadn't seen any cock, ringed or not, in nearly six years. That was the real crux of the problem. Of course he was hard now, with what was going on in the room down the hall. Because, despite his loud proclamations to the contrary, Matthew Silver had been living the monastic life since his banishment to the Cape all those years ago. Garry Kent, who had been the first, had also been the last.

Garry, Garry, Garry. Now there was one time where having a stiffy was very swell indeed. Just the recollection of that first time had Matt throbbing anew. Camp Wah-Tut-Ca in wintertime... a half-dozen boys gathered in a cabin just up the hill from the lake where they would swim come summer... all of them watching their two patrol leaders wrestling on the floor, choosing sides, chanting "Matty, Matty" or "Garry, Garry"... all of it in good fun, good fun that wouldn't be tolerated by the scoutmaster when he came back from wherever it was he was... and then there was the stiffy, the thick, hot slab of meat pressing against Garry's ass as Matt tried to hold him down. He was sure that Garry would out him to the group—"Silver's got a boner!"—but he didn't. Garry tapped the knotted wood floorboards, signaling his submission, and Matt stood up, victorious. Luckily, his khaki trousers billowed out in just the right way, hiding the evidence from the now-cheering crowd. But he couldn't deny what had happened with Garry, could he?

Garry clapped him on the shoulder. "Good match," he said, panting. And then he squeezed. Gently, but still a squeeze.

Later, gathering firewood from the back of Mr. Stern's over-sized van, that maroon behemoth which had conveyed the lot of them from the parking lot at Aldersgate Church in Chelmsford all the way up to the wilds of Northwood, Matt and Garry made small talk, and Matt thought he might be safe, thought that maybe Garry hadn't noticed. But then Garry asked, "Wrestling was exciting, huh?" and Matt knew that Garry knew, and Matt wondered if Garry knew that Matt knew that Garry knew.

A shrug was all that Matt gave him. "The younger kids seemed to enjoy it."

Garry leaned against the open van door. "Seemed like you enjoyed it, too," he said with a smirk.

"I'm sorry," said Matt, stuttering, his arms full.

And then there was another shoulder squeeze, this one firmer, more prolonged. "Don't be sorry," said Garry. "I enjoyed it, too."

And that was when the logs fell out his arms and onto the steel-toed boots Dad had just given him for Christmas, the steel-toes of which seemed to increase the pain rather than lessen it. Finally, something else throbbed in memory: his bare feet beneath the thin cotton sheet, a covering which seemed hardly enough now that he was traveling back in time, to another year, to another season entirely.

"You okay?" asked Garry, as he helped to collect the fallen logs.

"Are you...?" asked Matt, his face screwed up in pain both physical and mental.

"Don't look so disgusted," said Garry. "You are, too."

Was he really? Matt had wondered then, and he was

wondering again now. The only man he had ever been with was Garry. And with Garry, so much of it had been about the danger, from that first fumbling night at the back of Mr. Stern's van, where they'd exchanged nothing more than their confessions, to that last evening, in the spring, after their prom, when they'd ditched the girls they'd been obliged to bring by their parents, by the social code of their prissy little town, and come down here, down the Cape, just as Michael and Robin had tonight, to engage in a night of debauchery that they would never forget. Matt wondered if all he had really been after was the danger, the secrets, the lies. He wondered if he would still choose a man after all these years, or if the allure was gone. Grampy had accepted him for who he was, and the rest of the family knew now, even if they didn't approve. What was there left to drive him back to that aborted life he'd left behind all those years ago.

Nothing.

Matt lifted the pillow from his face. The house was silent, save for the occasional creak of a shutter in the wind. They were done, Michael and Robin. Matt reached beneath the covers, felt around. He was done, too.

THE NEXT MORNING, a copy of Susan Minot's *Monkeys* in one hand and a Tequila Sunrise in the other, Matt sat at the table of his blissfully quiet kitchen, at the back of his blissfully quiet house, and hoped that the blissful quiet would not be punctured at anytime soon by the grating laughter of chipper teenagers still riding the high of their sixth or seventh post-prom orgasm. He hoped that they had fucked themselves into a coma, if only a temporary one, and therefore it was with great dissatisfaction that he set down his book at the sound of the girl's voice. If not both of them in a coma, then why not her instead of Michael?

Michael he could deal with. Michael was blood. This girl, well she was another story.

"I've heard of liquid lunches," said Robin. "But liquid breakfast?"

Matt grinned at her, sipped from his glass.

"We didn't keep you up, did we?"

Matt shook his head. "No. Course not."

"Good," she said, searching the cupboards around the sink. "I got the feeling these walls were kind of thin."

"No," said Matt. "Grampy soundproofed the whole thing. Never knew where inspiration might strike. Wanted to be able to blow that horn of his anywhere he went, without waking anyone up."

"Really?" she said, sounding genuinely surprised. "Because we could hear all sorts of things from our room. Old pipes, squirrels in the attic, you name it."

"Oh," said Matt. "Well, I couldn't hear anything. Slept like a baby."

She nodded. "Anything to eat?" she asked.

"I'm a gay man, Miss Gates."

"And?"

"And, I don't like to work out. So, I don't eat breakfast. To compensate."

"You don't eat breakfast?"

Matt nodded, returned to his book. "Sacrifices must be made."

She began to search the cupboards again. Over the top of his book, when she wasn't looking, he watched her. On the back of her black t-shirt, running horizontally along the right side, were emblazoned the words 'further down the spiral', and for Matt, this said everything he wanted to say about where Michael was in his life, with this girl. The front of the shirt, a coil of rope which at first glance he had thought to be a puddle of orangey cat's vomit—they'd put anything on a t-shirt nowadays, right?— summed up his feelings nicely, too. It didn't matter whether it was the physical representation of the spiral alluded to on the back, or a puddle of bile and regurgitated fur; either way, her shirt got right to the gist of what Matt thought of her.

"Miss Gates," she repeated, some minutes later. "Oddly formal for the man who is supposed to be one of my boyfriend's best friends."

"I disapprove, if you haven't caught on."

She nodded as she poured a bowl of cereal for herself. He didn't bother to tell her that the Frosted Flakes had to be about a year old by now (they had been Grampy's favorite), or that the bowl hadn't been washed in nearly that long.

"It's just a little aggravating to know that my family is still associating with your family, even after—"

"Adam," she said, finishing Matt's sentence.

Matt nodded as she took a place at the table.

"What happened between my brother and Michael's sister was inexcusable."

"Inexcusable for whom?" asked Matt, finally setting his book down.

"For Adam, of course."

Matt sipped at his drink.

"Oh my God," she groaned, rubbing at her temples. "It's like nobody wants him to have fun. Ashley's on my case, and you, and... and the guys in the band."

"No," said Matt. "That's not what it is. He used to *be* fun, before our grandfather died. A little bit too serious at times, but a certifiable goofball if you got him in the right mood. He used to run around this yard, shadowing whoever had the video camera, and he used to ham it up whenever he got in front of the lens. Fake commercials, horrible knock-knock jokes, silly faces—"

"He has fun with me," said Robin.

"No, he doesn't. He's dark and gloomy and downright depressing. You bring out the worst in him. You amplify all those parts of his personality that don't need amplifying. Michael doesn't need black fingernails, or eyeliner, or songs about God being dead. He needs a partner who will remind him to be silly sometimes, to take a chance on smiling that awkward, beautiful smile of his every once in a while. He needs someone who will remind him that, despite the fact that our grandfather was taken away from us, that life is good, that life goes on."

"Partner," said Robin, sneering. "I see where this is going. You want a little gay buddy to go cruising through Provincetown with."

"I do not want a little gay buddy, Miss Gates." Matt laughed. "Michael couldn't handle homosexuality."

"You'd be surprised at some of things he can handle," said Robin, finally spooning the soggy flakes and skim milk into her mouth.

"I'm already surprised," said Matt, looking her over, standing up. "Your family hurts my family one more time, and you'll all regret it."

"Oooooh," she said, holding up her hands and feigning a shudder. "I'm shaking in my Chucks."

Matt turned away from her, and headed for the door.

✥

"IT'S AMAZING," said Michael, standing at the window. "Isn't it? That I'd end up with a girl like her?"

Matt grunted. He maintained a fixed gaze on the book in front of him, Morison's *A Maritime History of Massachusetts*.

Seemingly oblivious, Michael went on. "She is amazing in bed, Matt. Amazing. Nothing she won't try, and—"

"How would you know?" asked Matt, dog-earing the first page of chapter nineteen, 'Cape Cod and Cape Ann.'

"How would I know what?" asked Michael.

Matt leaned back in his chair. "How would you know if she's amazing in bed? What basis have you for comparison?"

Michael smiled and waved an admonishing finger at his cousin. "I've been with Betsy Fist and the Finger Sisters enough times to know what feels good. So don't try to pull that 'she's the only one you've ever been with' bullshit on me. I know I'm no Don Juan like you, but come on!"

"Michael," said Matt, "is this really the kind of girl you want to spend the rest of your life with?"

"The rest of my life?" said Michael. "Matty, I'm not thinking that far ahead."

"Well, you're setting a dangerous precedent. You keep on dating fast, loose women and soon that may be the only kind you—"

"Robin is not fast and loose," said Michael.

Matt arched an eyebrow, and Michael grinned in response.

"Okay," said Michael. "Maybe she's a little bit loose."

"Most Catholic kids are," said Matt. "At least nowadays. I know Garry was. Problem is, they think they can do anything they want to so long as they visit the booth on Sundays and tell their lurid tales to their pedophile priests. At least we WASPs know better. No matter how many Hail Marys you do, you're still going to have to answer for every blowjob, given or received, when you finally face the one guy who's opinion really matters."

"I'm not a WASP, Matty."

"Being a WASP's like being a Jew, Michael. You can't ever really stop."

"No," said Michael. "What I mean is—"

"Yes, I know what you mean, Michael. You think you're an atheist."

"I don't think, Matty. I know."

"Robin an atheist, too? That why you joined up?"

"I stopped believing the moment He took Grampy away."

Matt doubled over with laughter. "Michael... that's ridiculous. You stopped believing the moment *He* took Grampy away. Seems to me you still believe."

"The only reason human beings created God—"

"Oh, spare me!" said Matt.

"Why can't you be happy for me?" asked Michael.

"Why?" said Matt. He stalked across the room and grabbed Michael's hand. "You wore black nailpolish to your prom. And eyeliner, Michael. Fucking eyeliner! I didn't wear eyeliner to my prom Michael, and I'm fucking gay!"

"So what?" said Michael. "I'm daring to be different. That's the motto up at Kimball, in case you've forgotten."

"Oh, shove that in my face," said Matt.

"You could still go back someday."

"My ship has sailed, Michael. I'm past all of that, and all I'm trying to do here is help you get past it too."

"Robin makes me happy, Matty. I wish you, at least, could see that."

Matt put his arm around Michael, and walked him toward a portrait of old Silas the ninth. "Do you remember old Silas's story, Michael?"

"He had a dozen wives or something, right?"

Matt nodded. "He had a dream once, too. To be an actor, to have a life on the stage. He was in love with Shakespeare before the war. But when he came back, he was pressured into continuing on the family name. He was forced to give up any notion he had of a playful, adventurous life, and to get serious, to get down to business."

"And your point is?" said Michael.

Matt turned to face his cousin. "My point is that you're not being forced to do anything, at least right now. No one's forcing you to give up your painting—"

"The painting was going nowhere, Matty."

"—but you're doing it anyway. You're giving up your dream, and all I'm trying to say is that you're going to run out of time to dick around eventually. Just try to be sure you're dicking around in ways that matter to you."

"Robin matters to me. The band matters."

"To the kid I knew growing up, nothing mattered more than the painting."

"Well, maybe that kid is just as dead as God is," said Michael, stepping out from under Matt's arm. "Maybe that kid was nothing more than a fairy tale you told yourself to make yourself feel better about your own shortcomings. 'Oh, I can mold Michael into the new me,' or some shit like that."

"I was never trying—"

"Matty, as much as I wanted to be you growing up, some things just aren't possible."

"Michael, wait."

Michael waved goodbye, heading for the door, for the stairs. "We gotta hit the road. Robin's only a junior. She still has classes."

"OK," said Matt. "Drive safe."

From the office window, he watched them go, the old Ford Tempo rumbling up the hill, some dark electronic nonsense spewing forth from the sound system. "Hey God!" screamed the car's stereo. "Why are you doing this to me?"

"An atheist," said Matt, mumbling to himself, grinning. He shut the window, and went back to work.

ONE LAST TIME

These new townhouses, which his cousin hated, retained none of the character of the Cluster Houses which they now surrounded, and would someday replace permanently. Matt imagined them being plopped down by some random New England cyclone, the likes of which hadn't been seen since the Tornado of August 1851. All brick and mortar, they belonged to some distant kingdom, perhaps the realm of An, if not the land of Oz. In any case, they certainly were out of place here, amongst the brownish gray clapboard of the Cluster Houses. But, like all of the things that Matt's cousin Michael loved, Kimball College was being destroyed in the name of progress. *Sure,* Michael had said, *the Clusters are sinking into the ground a little more each year. But that... that's part of the charm.*

Matt had to laugh. The Clusters had had a certain appeal for him too, back when he was a prospective student, but he liked these new dorms just fine. Maybe it was his relative old age, or the design sense that had come as an added bonus with the purchase of his Gaydar, but he appreciated the poshness of these buildings quite a bit. They may not have had character, but they appeared to have all of the other perks you could want.

But they're going to tear down the Clusters because of these things, Michael had said. *And then the place where Jenna and I became Jenna and I will be gone.*

Matt laughed again. It was as if Michael thought that the old Cluster Houses were going to still be standing by the time he had kids and they were old enough to come back here. It was if Michael thought that his future children were actually going to care.

"What are you doing out here, pal?" asked a gruff voice.

Matt turned to identify his inquisitor. The campus safety officer was lean of body, save for the thick middle that seemed the birthright of all constables everywhere. His head was shaved bald, but in a precise way; not a hint of stubble was to be found up there. And his face was as smooth as his dome. Although, clenched in an all-business frown as it was, it couldn't properly be called handsome. His most memorable feature was his stare, a particular set to his eyes that seemed to proclaim he was going to get to the bottom of you, no matter what it took.

I hope he does get to the bottom of me, Matt thought, smirking. *After all, if this really is the last time, I want it to be a good one.*

"What's your business on campus, pal?"

"How do you know I'm not a student?" asked Matt.

"Less than five-hundred kids here. And I know every face."

Matt smiled. "I'm visiting my cousin. Michael Silver. Heard of him?"

The guard's face unclenched. "Good old Mikey's cousin, huh?"

"You know him?" said Matt.

"I know everybody," said the guard.

"So you must be the one he mentioned. The fudgepacker."

"Excuse me?!?"

"S'alright. We queers can call ourselves whatever we like," said Matt. "Or didn't you get the memo?"

The frown was back. Matt had a sudden vision of this guy living in his mother's basement. He ate chicken pot pies with the sad old maid, playing video games till four in the morning, wondering why he still hadn't kissed a girl yet. And then, one night, he woke up with a hard-on after falling asleep to the Sox locker room report, and suddenly he was like, 'Oh. *That's* why.'

"So," said Matt. "Are you?"

"I moonlight," said the guard.

"Well, rumor is Michael's left a room open for me if I want it. When do you get off?"

"I'm off now," the guard admitted, checking his watch.

"Well, my dear cousin certainly set this one up well," said Matt.

❧

"*THAT'S* DEATH," said Stanley, pointing at the blinking cursor. "To guys like you—writers, I mean—a blinking cursor on a blank page might as well be a bullet in the head."

Matt scoffed. "Oh my word. Everyone on this campus really is a drama queen. Even the campus security..."

"Campus *safety*," said Stanley.

"There's a difference?"

"Yeah, if I was *security*, maybe I'd get to carry a weapon."

Matt nodded his head. "Dubus wrote a story about you, about a townie turned campus rent-a-cop."

"Which Dubus?" asked Stanley. "Junior, or the old man?"

"The old man."

Matt felt an arm draped around his shoulder as he began to type again.

"'She died quietly,'" Stanley read aloud.

Matt sat back, enjoyed the feel of warm flesh against his own. "We're like the Village People, you and me."

"How's that?" asked Stanley.

"You're the cop, and I'm..."

"The Jew?" said Stanley, his hands rubbing at the knots in Matt's shoulders. "I don't think there was a Jew."

"I'm not Jewish," said Matt.

"Sorry. Figured with the last name..."

"Silver?"

"Silver does sound Jewish. You know, like David on *90210*?"

Matt laughed. "I'm a WASP, actually."

"I don't think there was a WASP, either."

"In terms of my analogy," said Matt, staring at the offending adverb on his screen, "I'm the Indian."

"The Indian?"

Matt backspaced until *quietly* was obliterated from his document. Then he deleted the whole sentence, leaving only the blinking cursor on the blank screen again. The best masseuse in the Bay State could not pull the tension away now.

"Great-grandfather messed around a bit," said Matt.

"Really?"

"Really," said Matt, retyping his sentence verbatim. He examined it again, and decided it would do. He smiled, took a sip of coffee.

"You know," said Stanley, "He's not the only gay cop in the world."

Matt put his mug down. "The guy from the Village People?"

"Yeah."

"Sure he is," said Matt, bending to rifle through his bag.

Stanley fell backwards onto the bed, groaning. "You think that, as a gay man, I would be better served by working in another field?"

"I think you'd look cute in a sailor's outfit," said Matt, arranging the three postcards he'd brought with him on the desk.

"What are those for?" asked Stanley. "*Correspondence*? You better mention the hot so-and-so you hooked up with while on vacation."

"They're rejection letters," said Matt.

Stanley sat up, and grabbed for them. "And you actually carry these things with you?"

"I travel light," said Matt. "But the things I bring with me, I bring everywhere."

"But why?" said Stanley.

"I have a little thing I do with them," said Matt, zipping up his bag, not wanting Stanley to peek around in there.

"What's that?" said Stanley, handing the cards back to Matt.

"You wouldn't understand," said Matt.

"What, I'm too stupid or something?" said Stanley, collecting his boxers from the floor.

"No," said Matt. "I'm the stupid one. And I do stupid things. What you wouldn't understand is why I do them."

"Oh," said Stanley, pulling on his pants. "Well, if you're ever up to visit again, and you feel like doing something stupid..."

Matt groaned. "I didn't mean..."

Stanley waved a hand dismissively. "I'm busting your balls." He smiled and shook his thumb at the door. "Gotta go before the rest of the house wakes up. I get caught in a dorm and I lose my job."

Matt stood, and they hugged. "There's always the navy," said Matt, as he gave Stanley a peck on the cheek.

"See you round," said Stanley.

"See you," said Matt.

৩১৩

HE COUNTED the letters one more time, just to be certain he knew how many bullets to load. The gun was on Michael's desk, the bullets beside it, and Matt was feeling a bit nervous about his chances. There were only six chambers, of course, and if his count was correct he'd have just two chances at salvation. But what if he didn't count the three from yesterday, and only took into account the one that he had found in the mailbox on the way out the door this afternoon? Those odds would be better.

Behind him, the door's combination lock clicked four times, and though Matt knew that meant his cousin was on the way in, he didn't bother hiding the gun.

"So, what did you think of..." Michael was saying, before his eyes keyed in on the desk, and opened big and wide.

"He was okay for a night," said Matt. "But I don't know if I could stomach his faux-machismo schtick for a whole—"

"ARE YOU FUCKING KIDDING ME?" said Michael, picking the .44 up off of the desk. "Are you fucking for real?"

"I told you about this. This summer."

"You told me you were fucking kidding, man."

"Well," said Matt, stumbling. "I wasn't."

"And you were going to do it right here, right here in my Goddamn dorm room?"

"I wasn't going to do anything," said Matt, pulling the gun away from his cousin and tossing it back into the bag. "I've been trying for six months, and I've never gotten the barrel anywhere even close to my head."

"Well that's comforting," scoffed Michael, plopping down onto his bed.

"I did shove it up my ass once," said Matt, with a straight face. "When all of my dildos were in the dishwasher."

Michael let loose a strained chuckle. "Loaded or unloaded?"

"Well, I *pretended* it was loaded. Does that count?"

Michael pulled a pillow over his head and mumbled something inaudible beneath it.

"Mikey," said Matt, putting a hand on his cousin's knee. "You gotta believe me. There are some things I've just got to do. It's all part of my process."

Michael sat up, tossed the pillow aside. "And you wonder why I don't want to be an artist anymore."

"You don't want to be an artist anymore because you've found something—or, in this case, someone—to distract you again."

"I thought you liked Jenna."

"I love Jenna," said Matt. "And you're a fool if you don't keep her around, but right now she's just a crutch for you, another excuse. Eventually you're going to have to look into the abyss just like I'm doing. You're an artist, Michael. And there's no escaping that."

"If being an artist means I have to put a fucking gun to my head every time a painting comes out like a piece of shit, then I'm done with it, Matt. I'm fucking done."

Matt smirked. "Maybe," he said. "But I guarantee it's not done with you."

❦

"AND HOW IS IT COMING TOGETHER?" Matt asked his cousin's girlfriend over breakfast the next morning. "The performance?"

Jenna didn't answer. She had a determined look on her face, but her eyes betrayed the fact that she was, mentally speaking, a million miles away.

"Jenna?" said Michael, a hint of aggravation in his voice.

"Huh?" she said. "What?"

"Matt asked you a question."

Matt waved his cousin off. "It's not a big deal, Michael. I was just making small talk."

"Well, it matters to me," said Michael. "You're our guest, and I would think she could tear her head away from the theatre for five minutes to actually participate in a conversation."

Jenna groaned, stood, and picked up her tray.

"Where are you going?" asked Michael.

"This is why I don't come to meals during hell week," said Jenna. "Nobody understands. I thought you would, but..." She turned on them, and stalked off.

A boy at an adjacent table turned and addressed Michael. "You're not doing your job properly, Mikey."

Michael groaned. "Oh, shut up, Andy."

Matt perked up at the sound of the name. So this was Andy, the old roommate. The old *gay* roommate.

"If you were doing your job, she wouldn't be so tense."

Matt chuckled, and Andy gave him a smile.

Andy picked up his tray and moved over to their table. "You must be Matt," said Andy, extending a hand.

Matt shook with Andy and nodded. Andy punched Michael in the arm with his free hand.

"Ow!" said Michael. "What was that?"

"I thought you said you were going to introduce us when you got him up here," said Andy. He turned to Matt. "Who did he hook you up with?"

"Stanley," said Matt, suddenly wondering if he'd remembered the name right. "I think."

Andy held a hand to his mouth and gasped. "He didn't?!? You hooked up with the skanky security guard?"

"When did you and I start talking again?" asked Michael.

"You must hate us both," said Andy.

"No," said Michael. "I was looking for someone who might complement Matt, complete him, not fuck him one night and write a stand-up routine about it the next."

"*Complete* him? Honey, you've seen *Jerry Maguire* one too many times."

"*Jerry Maguire?*" said Matt.

"You haven't seen it?" said Andy.

"He's a hermit," said Michael.

Matt frowned. "I prefer 'recluse.'"

"Well, anyway," said Andy. "That's what that fucking pretty boy Tom Cruise says to that Zellweger chick at the end of the movie."

"What've you got against Tom Cruise?" asked Matt.

"I could write a *book* about what I have against Tom Cruise."

"Don't get him started," said Michael, putting his head down on the table.

"The point is," said Andy. "Michael saying he wants to find someone to 'complete' you—that's a load of horseshit. It's the same thing as saying you 'love' someone."

"Whoa," said Matt. "What's wrong with telling someone you love them?"

"It's so fucking overdone," said Andy, with a sigh. "I mean, what does 'love' mean, anyway? And, as for 'you complete me,' do you know how many over-sappy, under-attractive men have tried to use that one on me since that movie came out?"

Matt smirked. "A lot?"

"You bet your fucking ass!" said Andy, standing up, working into a pitch-perfect Kinison impression. "I say, to hell with all this love and completion crap. Just come straight out and say you wanna fuck them and get it over with. The direct approach is so much more honest, and so much easier to deal with. If more men came up to me and said shit like, 'nice shoes, wanna fuck?' instead of this 'you complete me' bullshit, I'd be giving head a lot more often!"

Matt clapped at his apparent suitor's command performance, and gave a great hearty laugh. He cast a quick glance down at Andy's feet. "Nice shoes," said Matt.

Andy slapped a hand down on the table and chortled. "Now, that's what I'm talking about!"

Michael stood now, pulling his tray towards himself with a lurch, his half-full glass of Sprite toppling over.

"C'mon, cuz," said Matt. "Don't go all Bruce Banner on us."

"Your sister told me a couple of years ago not to bother with helping you out. I should have listened."

"C'mon, Michael..."

"Nah," said Michael. "I'm done. You don't want my help, then I'm finally gonna listen."

Michael marched across the dining hall and disappeared behind a divider near the kitchen.

"So," said Andy. "What about a one-morning stand?"

Matt looked across the length of the dining hall, waiting for Michael to reappear. But he didn't.

"Matt?"

"Sure," said Matt, shrugging his shoulders, figuring that one more time couldn't hurt. "Why not?"

CARL

Carl autographed a copy of *Sports Illustrated* for a hunchbacked old coot in a brown corduroy jacket and a blue Red Sox baseball cap. He shook the man's hand as he returned the magazine, and then he watched him skitter across the cavernous blue lobby of the multiplex. The old man shoved his prize into the face of a plump, silver-haired lady in a purple overcoat and pointed in Carl's direction. The woman sighed, squinted, and waved across the lobby at Carl. Carl grinned and waved back.

The cinema was quiet at the start of the business day. The sounds of the local light rock station seeped softly from the bevy of speakers that lined the walls. The smell of freshly buttered popcorn wafted across the lobby. And at the ticket counter, a solitary cashier was manning the register. The pimpled teenager was counting out the cash in his drawer, and Anna Simonson, in her manager's blazer, was hovering over him, checking the boy's work. Carl stared at his old flame.

Anna had long, straight blond hair and bangs cropped right above her eyebrows. Her skin stretched taut over her cheeks and under her chin. She had a small nose and small eyes and only her wide, thick lips gave her thin face weight. The curves of her body were, for the most part, hidden behind the straight lines of her dark blue blazer, which matched the color on the walls, but her breasts jutted outward in a stubborn refusal to be restrained by the bland uniform. She had never looked as good as she did that morning. In his memories and his daydreams, and in his old high school yearbook, she remained perpetually in sepia, but her beauty was best experienced in person, in full color. Carl reached into his suit coat and felt around the inside pocket for the small felt box, the gift he'd brought back from Cincinnati for her. When he found it, he clutched it in his hand.

The cashier finished counting and slid his drawer shut as Carl approached the register. Anna looked Carl's way for the first time, and she beamed. The cashier asked, "How may I help you?"

Anna folded her arms across her chest and stood up straight, waiting for Carl's response in silence.

"I've come to see about a girl," said Carl.

"I don't think we're showing that one," the cashier informed him, searching his computer screen to be sure.

Anna's face contorted. She held back a laugh.

The kid continued, "You want to see something else?"

"What would you recommend?" Carl asked, smiling at Anna as the kid began to recite the list of current attractions. Each of them, it turned out, was "wicked good," for one reason or another.

Anna tapped the cashier on the shoulder and cut his recitation short. "I think I'll handle this one, Chuck. Mr. Jacobson and I are old friends."

"Oh. I, uh..." the cashier stuttered, raising his gaze to meet Carl's. "You're him, huh?"

"I'm who?" asked Carl.

"The guy. The, uh..." The cashier paused, and smirked. "The football player."

"Go ahead and say it," said Carl, leaning across the counter.

"I don't know what you're talking about. Sir."

"I bet you don't," said Carl, growling as he stood straight again. "I've been back two hours and somebody wants to start this shit already."

Anna spoke. "Carl, maybe you should calm dow—"

"Say it! Go ahead! I hear ten times worse on the field every fucking Sunday."

The cashier moved to pick up the phone, but Anna clutched his shoulder. "That's enough," said Anna, taking the phone from him and setting it back in its cradle. "Mr. Jacobson and I will meet in my office."

Anna motioned for Carl to come around the corner and disappeared through a back door behind the counter. Carl started the way she had pointed but stopped when the cashier muttered, under his breath, "There are cameras all over the place."

"What did you say?"

The cashier snorted. "Just don't try anything. Everyone knows what you did to her."

Carl inhaled deeply, then continued around the corner.

He had succeeded in every aspect of his life except this. Women swooned at the sight of his dark, chiseled face, a gift from his mother. And men trembled at the sound of his booming, articulate baritone, the only genetic hand-me-down his long-dead father had left him. His tall, muscled body helped him bring home a sizable paycheck every Sunday. A new silver Cadillac sat in his garage back in Cincinnati, back where the rumors had not followed him, back where kids lined up in shopping malls, trading cards in hand, waiting for his autograph. But here, back home, people could not forget, would not. Except for old coots who didn't know any better, or didn't care.

Anna held her office door open, a somber half-frown on her face. She closed the door behind him, then wrapped her arms around his barrel chest, resting her head on his shoulder. Carl hugged her back and closed his eyes. He didn't realize he was squeezing too hard until she gently pushed against his ribs and stepped away.

"Easy there, big guy. I missed you too, but you don't want to break me in half, do you?"

Carl set his hand on the back of his neck and tried to knead the tension away. He cast his eyes downward.

"I'm sorry about Chuck," said Anna, as she sat on the edge of her desk. She motioned for Carl to have a seat on the leather couch she'd somehow managed to fit into the smallish room.

"That kid is a punk," he said. "Pure and simple."

"You know I've tried my best to put an end to all that stuff. Almost since the day it started."

Carl sank down onto the couch, its soft brown cushions yielding under his weight. He leaned forward, his upper body slouching toward Anna.

"It would be nice if you didn't let it get to you, though," she said. "Like you said, guys say things ten times worse on the field every Sunday, and you don't take their heads off."

"Well, actually, I do. Or, at least I try to," said Carl, grinning. "You know, all that tackling and wrestling each other to the ground... I'm not doing it because I like the smell of the other guy's sweat."

Anna laughed. "Listen. I thought we were doing dinner."

"Just couldn't wait to see you," he said.

Anna smiled. "Me neither." She stared at her watch. "I wish we could just run off right now. We have so much to catch up on. These phone calls and emails have been great but it's been..." She stared over at him. "Six years, right?"

Carl nodded.

Her eyes looked glassy, like she might cry. "I'll see you tonight though, right?"

"Absolutely," he said as they both stood up.

They wrapped their arms around each other to say goodbye, and though she did her best to muffle it in the folds of his coat, he heard her give a little whimper. Carl slipped his fingers through the river of her blond hair and rubbed her neck.

On his way out, Carl cast a murderous look at the cashier, waiting for a moment to see the kid's response, which was a pained expression—punctuated by a quivering lip—that made Carl think he'd just made the kid piss his pants. Satisfied, Carl stepped through the glass doors into the parking lot and headed for the car.

۞

HE DROVE ALONG CHELMSFORD STREET, away from the movie theater, heading toward his childhood home. All his life, until he was selected thirty-sixth overall by Cincinnati in the NFL Draft, he had lived in Chelmsford, Massachusetts. The town was an upper middle-class suburb of the old mill city of Lowell, and Chelmsford kids were taught by their parents to fear the filth of the neighboring city. Carl and his mom had lived right on the border.

With the top down on his rental, a warm April wind whipped along the smooth contours of Carl's buzz-cut head. He drove under the Route 3 overpass, out of Lowell and into Chelmsford. He gazed off to his left as he turned on his directional and pulled up to the stoplight. The old Route 3 Cinema, which sat on the corner of his street and the main drag, was boarded up now, closed when they'd opened Anna's shiny new movie house

Carl turned left onto his street and continued to cast glances at the derelict old building. He remembered his first date with Anna, who he'd been paired with when he couldn't stop burning his crepes in eighth grade Home Ec. During the following summer, the summer between middle school and high school, Anna's dad drove her over to the Jacobson apartment, and then Carl and Anna walked together down to the cinema to catch a movie. His sneakers stuck to the grimy floor, and he and Anna held hands in the back row. And then, just before the credits began to roll, they kissed for the first time.

Carl was startled to catch the size of his smile in the rear-view as he pulled into his mother's parking lot. He put the car in park and meandered across the lot, his eyes roaming about to take everything in. Many of the same cars filled the parking spaces, some more rusted. A modest conglomeration of trees surrounded the building and its lot, hiding it away from the sights, if not the sounds, of the main road. Back here, it was as if nothing had changed at all.

Carl hugged his mother with caution as he stepped into the old apartment, careful not to wrinkle her blouse, her gray skirt.

"I'm sorry I couldn't get this afternoon off," she said as she stepped away from him, as she pulled on a matching gray blazer. It gave her thin body just enough weight that it no longer seemed she would fly away in a breeze. "The district manager is coming in today, and I can't trust my store in the hands of my two bozo assistants."

"I wish you wouldn't work so hard," Carl told her.

The only slender daughter in a family of hearty, curvaceous, Italian women, she grew smaller and smaller every time he saw her. Her diet consisted primarily of Slim Fast milkshakes and Parliament Light cigarettes, and she spent almost all of her waking hours running the floor of a crazed, foundering department store. He was convinced she was going to work herself all the way into a coffin.

"I've got to pay the rent, Carl. I've got to pay the bills."

"I've told you. I'll buy you a house. I'll take care of you."

She scurried around the apartment, looking for something. "You know how I feel about that," she said.

"It's more money than I need, Ma. It's more money than anybody needs."

She returned to the living room, putting on her earrings. "I don't care, Carl. It's your money and I'm not going to leech off you. That just wouldn't be right."

"But you're my ma, Ma."

His mother rolled her eyes and shook her head. She stepped over to Carl and rose on her tiptoes to give him a kiss on the cheek. "I raised a good one, didn't I?"

"I do my best."

"Yes. Well, keep doing your best and keep bringing me out to that mansion of yours for Christmas, and that'll be enough." She looked around the apartment. "Where are my shoes?"

Cristina headed off toward her bedroom again. But this time, Carl followed her. "So, I'm going over to Anna's tonight for dinner."

"You mentioned that," she said.

"And you're not happy about it," grumbled Carl.

"I'm happy if you're happy, Carl."

"No you're not, Ma."

She slipped her shoes on, and now, thanks to her heels, stood closer to eye-level. "She could've stopped those rumors a long time ago, Carl. You've been dealing with that pain for too long and she could've stopped it right off the bat. But she didn't. And I don't have any respect for a girl who hurts my son. All these years of you pining over her..." His mother's voice stumbled. She sniffled. Cristina headed down the hall for the door, grabbing her pocketbook off the arm of the recliner.

Carl followed.

She faced him again, her voice pitched and louder. "That dedication you were supposed to do for that playground down the street, and then the whispers started and they had someone else do it. What about that?"

"It never hurt me as much as it hurt you, Ma."

She turned the latch and opened the door. "That, Carl, if you'll pardon my French, is bullshit." She paused and fumbled around in her purse for her keys.

"It's not bullshit. You... You can't leave on that note."

"I've got to go, Carl," she said, pulling her keys free from the tangle of beauty products and cigarettes.

"Ma, please? I don't want to go off tonight and be thinking about this fight."

"Then don't think about it, Carl." She scratched her nose, something she did whenever harsh words escaped her mouth without a dress rehearsal in her head. Carl had seen her scratch her nose a lot. "We'll see each other tomorrow," she said.

"Yeah. We'll do breakfast."

She closed the door behind her and Carl listened to her descend the stairs, each wooden step groaning and creaking, even under the small burden of her slight form. The sounds grew smaller and further away and everything was silent for a moment before the outside door swung closed with its particularly rattling crash.

❧

CARL ARRIVED at Anna's house that night with a bouquet of wild flowers in his hand and a fifty-dollar bottle of red wine under his arm. He waited at the side door in tapered beige slacks, a matching sport coat, and a shiny green button-down dress shirt, and wondered if he'd under- or over-dressed. He wasn't sure what she had in mind, and wasn't even entirely sure what he had in mind. He patted the breast of his coat to make sure the ring was still there.

Anna, for now, still lived with her parents in the same modest one-floor home she'd lived in since he'd met her. The house was bordered in the back by a small patch of woods and the Pine Grove Cemetery. Carl and Anna had made out in that small patch of woods once or twice, and getting drunk and roaming the cemetery on Halloween had been something of a tradition among their circle of friends during high school. One Halloween, some younger neighborhood kids came in and crashed the party. One of them, a greasy little black-haired punk named Bob Lee, had set about toppling tombstones. Carl thought about his father's grave across town and wondered if it was safe from kids like this. His jaw tightened, his shoulders tensed, and his friends backed away. Carl found the scrawny little shit roaming around a section of older stones with a bottle of Mountain Dew in one hand and a baseball bat in the other. Carl tackled him to the ground, throwing his own body as a spear into the kid's stomach and knocking him out cold. Carl's friends applauded his efforts, but Anna tried not to smile and then chided him for being too rough. She said something about her parents being friends with his parents, and that this was going to make things tense the next time they were invited over for dinner.

Carl didn't care. There were some things you just did not do.

Anna came to the door in an outfit far more satisfying than the dull work clothes she'd worn that morning. She wore a snug red cardigan with only two of its seven buttons buttoned. The neckline plunged all the way to her bust line and Carl found it hard to be a gentleman and keep his focus on her face. The two buttons below her breasts were fastened but the shirt flared open again to reveal her bare midriff, which, though it seemed to have grown a bit more round than he remembered, was sexy as all hell.

"Hey there," she said with a smile.

"Hey, yourself," he said. "You look great."

"I know," she said. "I'm trying to impress a guy."

"Really? Who is he?"

"I don't know if I should tell you. You might beat him up. You look like the kind of guy who might beat up the competition."

"Nah," said Carl. "I wouldn't hurt a fly."

Anna laughed and opened the door for him. "You want to come in?"

Carl stepped up into the doorway as Anna started in toward the dining room. He tried, with little success, to steal his eyes away from the sight of her hips and her bottom swaying in her low-rise jeans. It took him several moments to remember to close the door.

"Dinner's almost ready," she said from the dining room as he stepped up his pace to follow behind her.

Soft candlelight filled the dining room and two gleaming dinner plates were set opposite each other on the small round table. Carl had never seen those plates used. He'd only ever seen them inside her mother's China cabinet.

Mellow piano music drifted in from the living room stereo. Anna peeked around the corner from inside the kitchen and asked him, "You want to bring those flowers in here so we can get them in some water?"

Carl set the wine down on the table and headed for the kitchen with the flowers. "I guess this answers my question," he said.

She took the flowers from him and asked, "What was your question?"

"I wondered whether or not this was a romantic thing or just a just-friends thing."

"Oh. So you realized it was a just-friends thing then? That's good." She smiled at him over her shoulder and she stuffed the flowers into a tall porcelain vase.

Carl took the vase from Anna and went back into the dining room, chuckling to himself on the way. He took off his coat, draped it over the back of the chair, and sat down.

Anna wore a different oven mitt on each hand as she carried a steaming pot in from the kitchen. One was Christmas-themed, adorned with the figure of Santa Claus—all red and white—while the other was a holdover from Halloween, green on one side, orange on the other, with tiny cartoon pumpkins sewn in here and there.

"Do you like my fashion statement?" she asked as she set the pot down in front of him.

"I do," he said. "It makes this all feel so much more comfortable. It's not like you're trying to impress me."

"Cooking for you isn't impressive?"

"That's not what I meant—"

She ran the hand in the Halloween mitt gently down across his face, from his forehead to his chin. "I know what you meant, silly."

Carl spooned linguine out of the pot and onto Anna's plate, then his own.

Anna ventured into the kitchen again. "I bet your girlfriends back in Cincinnati wouldn't be caught dead in clashing oven mitts."

"Well," he said. "To be honest, they wouldn't be caught dead in an oven mitt at all, let alone two."

Anna brought back a small saucepan and a foil tray full with chicken, tomato sauce, and melted cheeses. She set them down and then sat down herself.

Carl watched her fight to get the oven mitts off, each gloved hand struggling to grip the other. "I thought I'd told you I didn't have any girlfriends back home," he said. "It didn't feel right to be talking to you on the phone and on the computer and then having another relationship on the side. You know, I thought it might be like cheating."

Anna turned to Carl and held out her hands. "You mind ungloving me?" she asked.

He took hold of her right wrist with one hand and pulled the mitt off with the other. She pulled off the second mitt on her own.

"Thank you," she said.

"You're welcome."

Anna surveyed the table, looking puzzled. "Need to get some water," she said, getting up again.

"I brought wine," Carl reminded her.

The faucet came on in the kitchen. She replied, "I know. I don't think I'm going to drink this time."

"Fair enough," said Carl, scooping a piece of chicken out of tray and onto his plate as Anna returned with a pitcher of ice and tap water.

Anna's meal reminded Carl why she had been the star pupil in Home Ec. and why the teacher had paired her talent with his sorry ass. He felt full as he stared across at her, as she continued to binge on pasta and sauce.

She placed her fork down on the emptied plate and dabbed around her mouth with her napkin. She'd missed a tiny speck of sauce on her chin and he wasn't sure if he should tell her.

"You're wondering where I put it all, aren't you?" she asked.

"Nah. When you cook that good you're allowed to stuff yourself on it."

Anna pushed her seat back from the table and stood. Carl followed her lead as she asked him, "You want to head in the other room?"

They stepped out of the dining room and into the shadowy living room. Candlelight flickered from atop the entertainment center and from the imitation oak coffee table and the shelves built into the wall. The aroma was a mix of summer berries, lilacs, apples, and cinnamon.

Anna sat sideways on the couch and patted the cushions for Carl to sit with her. He sat and faced her, and when she took his hands in her own he inched closer. He realized he didn't have the ring, that it was still in the other room.

She looked down into her lap. "I have something to tell you," she said.

Carl was silent.

Still not looking at him, she said, "I've been seeing someone."

Carl swallowed and sighed. He hoped he wasn't sweating. "There's nothing wrong with that, I guess. I... I guess I was taking things too seriously. We've only been talking on the phone and emailing, after all. I mean, we haven't been us in years."

Now she looked at him. "Could you be quiet while I finish?"

"Yeah," he said.

"Bob Lee," she said. "I've been seeing Bob Lee."

Carl let go of her hands and tried to rub away the throbbing and the heat that the mention of the name had brought upon his forehead and temples.

"Are you just gonna freak out," she said, "or are you going to let me explain?"

"Of all the people in Goddamned world, it had to be him. It had to be him, didn't it?"

Anna put her hand on his knee and words had begun to cross her lips as Carl stood and backed up away from her.

"Do you even remember the kind of things that kid did in high school? Do you remember the night in the cemetery?"

"A lot has changed since high school, Carl."

Carl walked out of the living room, through the dining room, and headed for the door. Anna's boot heels clicked on the linoleum as she rushed up behind him.

"I never mentioned it because I've been thinking about ending it the whole time."

Carl stopped short of opening the door. He faced her.

"Ever since I got that first email from you," she said, "I've been thinking of ending it. Bob and I had been together for a couple of years. Our parents were thrilled, of course. But there wasn't any spark there, Carl."

She was sweating. Carl watched the perspiration bead up along her forehead. The speck of sauce she'd missed on her chin had been driven off.

"Bob's in the army now, got the call about two months ago. I was going to do it before he left. You know... I was going to end it. But... then something happened." She paused and said not to him, but to her stomach, "I'm pregnant."

Carl trembled. He began to sweat himself. He felt it gathering underneath his arms and in the small of his back. "Why all this, then? Huh? Dinner? Candles? Is this some joke?"

Anna's skin was losing color. She breathed deeply and steadied herself, gripping onto one of the chairs. She pulled the chair away from the table and sat down.

"Is it some joke, Anna? Tell me—Cause I don't get the punch line yet. I don't get the punch line."

"No. It isn't a joke, Carl. It's not a joke." She stopped, and picked up the glass of water she'd had with dinner. She sipped at it. The dim light glimmered across her wet eyelashes. "I asked you to come back because I want to be with you."

"You want to be with me? How?" he screamed. He breathed deep for a moment, and then lowered his voice. "How can you be with me? You're having his baby!"

"Let me explain—"

"No! You let me explain. You think it's not bad enough already that everyone in this town thinks I raped you back in high school? Now you want me to be the arrogant son of a bitch celebrity who came back home just to steal away the local schlub's girl, and his kid too?"

"You didn't rape me," she said, setting down the drinking glass and wrapping her arms around herself.

Carl stared at her stomach.

"I couldn't do it, Carl. I tried to do it, but he came over, and Bob... he was never anything but nice to me. You know? He had this whole romantic dinner planned and then, afterward, he starts kissing me—"

"I don't need to hear this."

Anna sniffled. "I woke up the next morning and he was gone... didn't leave a trace he'd ever been there." She rubbed her stomach. "Except this."

"Has he called you? Written? Anything?"

She shook her head in a silent 'No.'

Carl rubbed his forehead and ran a hand across the stubble on his scalp. He pulled another chair up close to her and sat in it. He opened his arms and she leaned into him. He felt the heat of her face as her tears seeped through the thin fabric of his shirt and onto his chest.

"Are you going to keep it?" he asked her.

She stared up at him and said, "It depends on your answer."

Carl let her go and she wiped at her eyes with her bare hands. Mascara had streaked down across her cheeks, and her wiping was only making it worse. Carl asked, "You want me to help you raise it?"

"Yeah," she said. "I want to keep it but I don't want to do it alone. You and I have been talking and it's been just like old times. I always imagined being with you in the end." Anna sniffled. "I guess I'm just hopeless and romantic, huh?"

He let his hand rest against her cheek and rubbed a tear away with his thumb. Carl stood. "I don't have an answer for you," he said. "Not yet."

"That's fine," she said, rising out of her chair to stand with him. "I'm just glad you stopped yelling. There's a reason our grandmothers called this a delicate condition, you know."

They walked together to the door. Carl treaded slowly down the three steps to the driveway. Anna stood at the door for a moment and then she stepped out of sight.

Carl sat in his car for ten minutes, in the dark, mulling over the decision in his head. He considered driving off, sleeping on it, and telling her in the morning. He saw a curtain open slightly, saw Anna peering out in a pair of flannel pajamas. And then, behind her, Carl saw his jacket, still draped over her dining room chair, the small felt box still resting at the bottom of the inside pocket. He leaped out of the car, raced to her door, and knocked.

IAN

A dreadful numbness had swallowed Ian Ipsum's body from the waist down. Though his eyes had been open for an hour, he had not yet moved. Falling asleep in his creaky office chair had not been the most brilliant of ideas. The luminous glow of his computer's monitor lit his plump face, his disheveled mass of pavement-black hair, his unshaven chin and gullet. Before nodding off, he'd reached page six of six in his Internet job search. He'd found nothing.

Ian looked down at his bulging gut, which, with every breath he took, forced the retractable keyboard shelf back under the wooden desk. He looked at his thighs—big, white, hairy whale thighs that never seemed to grow smaller, no matter how many miles he logged on his exercise bike. Ian shook his head in disgust and gripped the armrests of his chair to push himself up. He whimpered, then gritted his teeth as he strained to stand. Sweat trickled down his forehead, down the bridge of his nose. He trudged across the worn taupe carpet of his one-bedroom apartment, toward the kitchen, to make something to eat.

He wheezed as he went. The apartment's previous occupant had been a six-packs-a-day smoker. She'd succumbed to emphysema on the living room carpet a week before Ian had moved in. There was still a bloodstain there, where old Mrs. Davis had coughed up what was left of her last cancerous lung. Ian's mother had covered the spot with a potted fern when they moved him in, but the plant had perished within a week and every replacement that he'd picked up from the K-Mart down the street had wilted away as well.

The walls and carpet had absorbed every puff Mrs. Davis had ever taken, and seemed reluctant to let go of her memory. Ian and his mother had attacked the apartment with Febreze—sixteen bottles of it—and it had done nothing. Pine tree air fresheners, the kind you bought out of vending machines at the car wash— they hung on multi-colored pushpins. And he owned no fewer than a dozen Glade Plug-Ins. Each and every electrical outlet in the place had been co-opted.

The apartment building, a retrofitted Victorian sided with rotting gray cedar shingles, sat in the armpit of the Merrimack Valley, a tiny patch of wooded, swampy flatland on the border of Lowell and Dracut, Massachusetts. The building was a part of quiet, suburban Dracut by zip code only. The dank building, its pothole-infested parking lot, and the deafening gangsta' rap that poured out of the neighbors' crack dens—that was Lowell, the city, the slum his parents, who lived in the upper-class suburb of Chelmsford, had always warned him about. The building wasn't connected to a fire department in either town. If it were set ablaze, it was up to the residents themselves to call into town and request their rescue.

Ian's stomach rumbled in protest as he gathered the ingredients for his meal—the vile protein shake prescribed to aid in his weight loss campaign. From the refrigerator, he brought a half-empty bottle of high-pulp orange juice and a small packet of the orange-flavored fish-oil supplement he'd scoured the Merrimack Valley for an hour and a half to find. From the cupboard above the sink, where he used to store family-sized boxes of Twinkies and

Devil Dogs, he took a massive canister of whey protein and a thin tube of powdered fiber. Neither Ian, nor his tongue or stomach, were looking forward to this. But he had begun to reap rewards from the prescription. He was down to two hundred and ninety pounds. Progress sure didn't taste good, but it was progress just the same.

Besides, the ice cream truck was on its way and he didn't have a moment in which to dilly-dally. The truck arrived at the same time every afternoon, parking outside his window and belching its music across the small basin in which his apartment building sat, the notes of 'Turkey in the Straw' bouncing off the surrounding hills. Ian needed to get something into his belly before it arrived to play the part of pied piper, before it tried again to lure him outside, away from progress—before it stopped his forward motion with mounds of rocky road.

The phone rang as Ian was pouring orange juice into the blender. He stepped across his cramped kitchen and picked the cordless up off its cradle on the wall. "Hello," said Ian.

"Hello," came his father's voice. "You just wake up?"

"I've been up an hour," Ian told him, scooping powdered whey protein into the mix.

"It's noon. You got up at eleven?"

"I was up late," Ian explained, sealing the whey protein canister and searching the countertop for his measuring spoons.

"Doing what? Looking at porn?"

"Looking for a job, Dad. You know I work better at night."

"Sitting at your computer staring at the damned Internet all night is not work. If you really want a job you need to get your ass out of bed on time and you need to get out there and hit the streets. Pound the pavement. Knock on doors. Make phone calls when people are actually in the office." His father paused, sighed. "You're hopeless you know..."

Ian said nothing. He poured four tablespoons of fiber supplement into the heap of powder and juice. He knew that his father wasn't through with his diatribe.

"...and you've wasted two years of your life away out there in California, pursuing some ridiculous dream, only to come home broke and filch off your mother some more. Do you have any idea how much of our savings she's wasted on you? On your damned apartment? On that phone line you're using to cruise the triple-x sites all night long? Do you have any idea what kinds of lies she's been telling to hide it from me?"

Ian ripped open the small packet of fish oil supplement and squeezed the thick orange paste into the blender. His father continued, but he wasn't listening. Ian put the top on his blender and pressed his finger down upon its button. The machine growled to life, its grinding racket filling the room. Ian could no longer hear a word his father was saying. And for the first time all morning, he smiled.

When he'd graduated from Kimball College with a theater degree two years ago, his father had told him to take advantage of the thriving job market while he could. Ian had dreams of moving to Hollywood, of making it big, and his father apparently felt it was his duty to temper those dreams with harsh doses of reality. For a graduation present, he'd bought Ian biographies of James Dean, Elvis Presley, Marilyn Monroe, and a book on the Black Dahlia murder case, and he'd dog-eared the sections that described each horribly tragic death. Ian's mother, who was more supportive —or simply less disapproving—bought him a plane ticket. He flew from Manchester, New Hampshire into LAX two weeks later.

But the highest Ian had ever made it on the Hollywood food chain was when he served as a seat-filler at the Academy Awards, sitting beside Maria Shriver while Arnold Schwarzenegger, he presumed, was taking a dump. Dad, he was now willing to admit, had probably been right.

The whole of his middle contracted around the empty cavern

of his stomach. Ian doubled over and held on to the counter's edge to keep from collapsing. All that was left in him was acid and bile, and it had begun a swift, determined march up his esophagus. Ian turned the blender off and pulled a tall glass out of the strainer.

His father was still ranting. "...focus and determination, Ian. That's what it's about—focus and determination. You don't want to be fat forever, do you?"

Ian mumbled, "No, Dad." He poured the shake into his glass.

"All right. That's a start."

Ian heard the ice cream truck making its approach, descending the hill into his wooded and swampy dead end. Ian grimaced and stumbled towards the kitchen window, phone in one hand and shake in the other. Aftershocks rippled from behind his bellybutton into his thick love handles. He hadn't sipped from his drink yet. It splashed over and slipped down the sides of the glass.

"Ian? Are you listening to me?"

The truck's music blared as it pulled up to the edge of the forest opposite Ian's building.

"I'm listening, Dad. It's just that this ice cream truck—"

"An ice cream truck? You're pathetic, Ian. You're—"

"Who cares if I'm overweight, Dad? Who fucking cares?" Ian snapped. "I could still be the next Chris Farley, the next John Candy."

"Yeah, maybe. But John Candy was funny. You're just fat."

Ian shrieked and hurled the phone across the small room. It made a crunch and left a blackened dent in the wall, then fell, bounced, and snapped in half. The battery pack popped out and skidded across the faux-linoleum flooring, sliding underneath the refrigerator. Ian threw his shake towards the sink and missed. It hit the wall and shattered, glass and orange slime crafting a fluorescent Rorschach. The next-door neighbor banged on the common wall.

Ian stomped his way out of the kitchen, into the hallway, and then he flew down the two flights of stairs that led to the outside. He rumbled out the glass door and then across the thick, uncut grass. The boxy, white ice cream truck stood just a lane and a half of pavement away. It was covered with placards advertising cones stacked three scoops high, in a variety of alluring flavors. His mouth watered. There was orange sherbet and lime and lemon. There was vanilla soft-serve, chocolate, vanilla and chocolate twist. Smaller cards were spread across the façade as well. One promoted vanilla and chocolate ice cream on a stick, shaped in the form of a cartoon dog's head. Ian's stomach growled, though not in anger this time. Give me some of that, it seemed to say.

Heat pulsed up from the blacktop and sweat collected in the crease behind his knees. It was only at this moment that Ian realized he was still wearing nothing more than an extra-large Bart Simpson t-shirt—*Don't Have a Cow, Man*—and red flannel boxer shorts. He hadn't even bothered to put on any shoes.

Ian scampered across the rest of the street and banged his fist against the service window.

The window slid open, and a pretty girl leaned down to take his order, her low-cut, loose-fitting UMass Lowell t-shirt sagging to reveal a modest measure of cleavage. Her short, curly hair was the color of peanut butter. Her skin was the golden brown of French toast on a Sunday morning. Square-rimmed glasses sat low on her significant nose.

"That is quite the fashion statement," she said, looking him over. "I don't know if they told you, but Bart Simpson is sooooooo over. And red plaid—that is just not your color."

Ian clenched his right fist, felt his untrimmed fingernails cut into his palm.

"Can I help you?" she asked, giggling.

"Sundae," he said. "Hot fudge. The works."

"Sure," she said and then paused. The girl looked him once over and then stood. She dug through the pockets of her hip-hugging blue jean cutoffs. Ian spied a sliver of her midriff. She pulled a folded pink index card from her front pocket and leaned back down to meet his gaze.

"That a recipe?" he asked.

She stared alternately at him and at the card. "How much do you weigh?" she asked.

"Why does that matter?" Ian huffed. "You're really going to get on me because of my weight. I'm a paying custom..." Ian trailed off. "Shit," he said. "I left my wallet inside."

"How much do you weigh?" she repeated.

"You suck."

"Tell me how much you weigh, and maybe I'll give you a free sundae."

"Two-ninety," Ian grunted. His feet were beginning to burn. He shifted from one foot to the other. "You satisfied now?"

The girl took one last look at the card. "Perfect," she said. "Come around back, through the service door."

Ian bounded around the back of the truck and sighed in relief as he stepped onto the soft, moist mud on the other side. He watched the door slide open. The girl waved him in.

"Come in," she said. "Have a seat."

He stepped up into the truck, the metal beast creaking under his weight, and then he sat Indian style in the small open space between three large silver and white coolers. The corrugated steel floor was sticky with the residue of a hundred thousand ice cream cones, but also comfortingly cold.

"Could you shut that door, please?" his hostess asked, as she ran an ice cream scoop under the faucet of her small sink.

Ian slid the door shut behind him. He turned and watched the girl bend over one of the cases of ice cream. While she scooped three scoops of vanilla into a plastic dish he stared at her small, firm bottom, trying to determine if she was wearing any under-wear. He had no luck.

"I'm Bette, by the way," she said as she drizzled hot fudge over the sundae.

"Ian," he said.

She sprinkled chopped nuts. "What do you do, Ian?"

"Right now I'm just looking for a job," said Ian, wiping sweat from his forehead. "I was out in California for a while, working as an actor."

"Been in anything I would've seen?" Bette asked, dispensing whipped cream, cherries.

"Uhm... No. Probably not."

"Are you still looking for acting jobs then? Even back here in Dracut?"

"No, I... uh... uhm—"

"You're quite an elegant speaker, Ian. I'm surprised you don't get more gigs."

Ian slouched and stared down at his bulging, perspiring midsection. "You sound just like my father," he said.

Bette sat down in the small space opposite him and held his sundae in her lap. "I'm just playing around. I'm sure you're a great actor."

"I appreciate the lip service," he said, "Can I have my ice cream now?"

"Not yet," she said. "I'm going to make you an offer you can't refuse."

"What's that?" he asked. His stomach grumbled, loud enough that she couldn't have missed it. "Does it involve me getting my ice cream?"

"It involves you, and me, and that very anxious part of you that's hanging out of your boxers."

Ian looked down at his crotch and covered himself with his right hand, stuffing himself back inside the folds of his underwear.

Bette laughed. "Are you a virgin?"

Ian felt his lower lip sag as he remembered his last night out west, when he had paid to lose his virginity to a tall redhead with grotesquely long purple fingernails.

"Yes," he answered.

Bette pulled one of the cherries off the top of his sundae and placed it between her teeth. "You mind?" she asked, but before he could answer she bit down hard on it, its juices splattering onto her thin pink lips.

"You want to have sex with me?" said Ian, eyeing his dessert.

"It's a sorority thing, okay?"

"What sorority? What's the thing?"

"I'm rushing Eta Omicron Epsilon."

Ian looked longingly at his ice cream. It was starting to melt. "What's the thing?" he repeated.

"I... well, I have to fuck a fat kid. A virgin, preferably"

"Oh," said Ian.

"So, you know, you scratch my back and I'll scratch yours —right?"

"I'd just like my ice cream if that's all right," said Ian. "I, uh, if you need me to go get some money—"

"Fine," she said, shoving the dish towards him, not letting go easily when he tried to pull it from her.

Ian spooned heaping dollops of the sundae into his mouth, devouring the first half of the dessert without even tasting it. But then he slowed himself. He slurped another spoonful into his open maw and closed his eyes. He tried to shut out everything else but the taste of the ice cream on his tongue. The hum of the truck's motor and its obnoxious song; the feel of the cold, gummy floor—it all melted away. The mixture of vanilla and fudge and nuts spread across his tongue and his palate. It tasted like childhood. It brought him back to that time when being pudgy was endearing, and not terrifying.

There was a shift then, in the truck's weight. Ian opened his eyes and saw Bette standing. Her top was gone, her small tanned breasts firm, tempting—like two scoops of coffee ice cream, each with their own small cherry on top. She had unbuttoned her cutoffs and was pushing them to the floor. When she stepped out of them, all that was left to cover her was a thin landing strip of hair, darker than the tresses atop her head, more chocolate than peanut butter.

"What are you doing?" Ian asked, his mouth full again with ice cream.

"I'm going to convince you," she said.

"How's that?"

Bette pulled the ladle from the vat of hot fudge. The gooey chocolate oozed over the sides. Bette threw her head back and arched her spine. She tipped the ladle and let sauce dribble down her shoulders, her neck, over each of her mouth-watering breasts.

Ian felt himself drooling.

Bette went down on her knees, hot fudge still trickling down the length of her, and she lay back as far as she could. From the counter, she collected the can of whipped cream and then sprayed a crude arrow along her midsection.

Ian set the ice cream on the floor and pulled his dick through the flap of his boxers. She moaned softly as he mounted her, as he licked her clean and pumped away. It was an act, he was sure, but it was an act he was willing to suffer.

When they were done, she held him inside of her and she pulled a camera from a backpack she'd stowed under the counter. They each snapped a couple of pictures from their respective angles and then she took one of the two of them together from arm's length.

She gave him a kiss on the cheek and said, "Thank you," as he stepped out of the truck.

Ian wondered, "Does this thing play any other songs?"

"What's a matter? You don't like my jingle?" she asked, grinning and then sliding the door shut.

Ian crept across the hot pavement, covered in vanilla ice cream, hot fudge, whipped cream, and in Bette's own sweet juices.

He stepped onto the grass and the cool of lawn soothed his feet. Ian headed for his apartment.

"You have no willpower at all, do you?" came his father's voice.

Ian looked up. His father stood at the door, about to ring the bell, with two plastic Wendy's bags in his hands. Ian's dad was even larger than Ian himself, a roly-poly man in enormous blue jeans and a white New England Patriots t-shirt that barely covered his bulging beer gut.

"What's in the bag?" Ian asked.

"Couple of salads," said Ian's father, staring away from his son. "But, seeing as you've already eaten..." Ian's dad shook his head and started back towards the parking lot.

"Dad! Wait," said Ian, running after him, catching him just as he reached his weathered green four-by-four, panting from the exertion. "You don't understand, Dad," Ian told him.

But Ian's father didn't listen. He stepped up into the truck, tossed the two salads into the passenger's seat, and looked down on Ian as he closed the door. Then he pulled away without saying a word.

۞

AFTER A SHOWER THAT EVENING, Ian stood naked in his bedroom, in front of a long mirror, and he stared at the soiled clothes piled in a heap at his feet. He looked at his reflection, and he slapped at his undefined pecs, his man tits. They bounced up and down, the jerking movement of their heft making him wince. His chest grew pink, then red, then a subtle shade of purple. Ian squeezed the rolls around his stomach tight, so hard that he began to cry. "Look at you, you fucking fatass," he said to himself. His dick was growing hard again, the song of the ice cream truck playing in his mind. He was both hungry and horny. Ian wiped at his eyes and headed for the kitchen, to try and ease at least one craving.

By the bright light of the opened refrigerator door, he scoured cupboards, the freezer, and the fridge itself. All he could find was a bag of semisweet chocolate chips, left over from the days before the diet. He found it wedged behind jars of kosher dill pickles and low-carbohydrate marinades. Ian sat in the dark, on the kitchen floor, his head resting against the wall, and he tore open the bag. Ian poured a handful of the chips into his hand, and then shoved them into his mouth. He chewed and swallowed, then took another handful, and another.

And another.

TOMORROWLAND

The roller coaster came to a full and complete stop just after they'd slid past the loading area and the control booth, just as they'd descended the small slope that would take them into the ride proper. Ahead of their train, Veronica saw the tunnel of pulsing blue lights grow suddenly dark. She heard the sounds of the Space Mountain "energy surge" fade into silence. And then she turned around in her seat, as best she could with the T-bar restraint keeping her in place, and she asked her cousin, "What the hell is going on here?"

Michael shrugged and said, "Dunno."

The overhead lights came on, washing out the attraction's eerie ambience. A few moments later, one of the ride attendants came bouncing down the set of stairs just to the left of their vehicle, a heretofore invisible set of steps which descended down the slope and into the now bright white light of the tunnel.

"What's going on?" cried Veronica to the attendant.

"Nothing to be worried about, m'am," he said with a smile. "You'll be on your way shortly."

Veronica groaned.

"Chill out," said Michael. "I'm sure they'll figure it out soon."

Veronica held her left arm up, twisted her wrist back and forth. "You see what time it is, Michael?"

"Oh, Jiminy Cricket," said Michael. "Not the damn schedule again."

"We're supposed to be leaving for the next park in twenty minutes, and we haven't even gotten in line for Dumbo yet, let alone ridden the stupid thing."

"If you were that concerned about Tracy getting to ride flying elephants, why didn't you have Des and Jenna take her over there while we were in here?"

"Because I want to see her on the ride," said Veronica. "You don't understand, Michael. Getting your kid on all the rides she wants to ride is only part of it. The other part, the bigger part, is being there to watch her enjoy them. That's what makes the interminable flight and the hellish heat and the exorbitant price of the watered-down soda all worth it. Otherwise, what's the point?"

"I think the point is to enjoy yourself," said Michael. "But, I mean, if you didn't want to ride this ride, we could've—"

Veronica turned her head to look him in the eye as best she could. "I wanted to ride Space Mountain, Michael. It was the one thing I wanted to do for myself. I've told you that."

"Okay," said Michael. "I'm just saying... If you wanted to do Dumbo instead, we could've come back another—"

Veronica sighed and turned away from him again.

"What is it about Space Mountain anyway?" asked Michael. "You've avoided every other thrill ride in the place."

This was true, Veronica thought to herself. She was much more of a "It's A Small World" kind of girl than a "Big Thunder Railroad" chick. But there was something about Space Mountain, something she wasn't quite sure she could articulate to Michael, not because it was all that difficult to explain, but because it sounded so silly when she explained it to herself.

Summer trips to Disney World had been something of a tradition for Michael's family. They'd gone four times that Veronica could remember, and they had the overstuffed photo albums to prove it. But for Veronica's family, the Disney experience had been a one-time thing. It was 1988, the summer before the Great Schism. Mom and Dad were doing their best impression of a happy couple, even carrying their act into the evening so that, after the first night, Veronica didn't bother to stay awake waiting for the sounds of their fighting to break through the thin hotel walls. Matt's performance wasn't so convincing, at least not to Veronica, who saw the glum expression that he wore at night, saw the ghost of that glumness in his face even when he smiled and played the part of the favorite son during the day.

Her most solid memory of that week—the rest of it was a blur of bright colors and the cheery sounds of children at play—was of the ride she and Matt took on Space Mountain, and of the aftermath of that ride.

She supposed now, with the power of hindsight at her command, that she should have known what was going on between the ride attendant and her brother as they snaked forward through the line. She remembered how odd it seemed to her that they kept staring at each other, but she also remembered writing it off as nothing more than boyish machismo.

'You nervous?' her brother had asked her once, or twice, or a half a dozen times. And now she realized, again through hindsight, that it had been as much a question for himself as it had been for her. As the attendant directed them to their car, there had been one last look shared between the two boys. And then Matt was back to his old sullen self. He made his way up front, and she sat behind him. They'd lost track of Mom and Dad, who'd probably been shunted off into a train on the other side.

It wasn't until they'd descended the slope, made their way through the tunnel of flashing blue light, and rocketed into the ride proper that Matt changed, changed for the moment, and for good. As they rocketed through the darkness at thirty miles per hour, she heard a distinct change in his screams. They went from shrill yelps of terror to deep, guttural, almost primal bellows. He'd lost it. That's what she'd thought at the time. He'd flipped his lid. Matt screamed, 'That the best you got?' as they hurtled down an unseen drop.

Veronica felt as if the very soul of her had lifted up out of her body for a moment, as they tumbled down, a heavy, leaden weight rising up out of her stomach and into her throat. And, for a moment, she was lost to the world. But then that weight came crashing back down into her, and she was back in that car, with her screaming sibling in front of her, and, try as she might to scream, she couldn't make a sound.

When they found Mom and Dad again, out in the center of Tomorrowland, Matt, breathless, told the lot of them that he was going back, that he wanted to ride it again.

It wouldn't be until later that night that Veronica would get the truth out of him. There had been no second ride. Instead, there had been a stolen kiss in a Tomorrowland bathroom, and a promise to meet up again before the week was over. Matt came back to the hotel room that night and confessed to Veronica what he was. 'I like guys,' he'd said. 'And there's no use denying it anymore.'

'Does this have anything to do with all that screaming you did on Space Mount—'

'Yes,' he'd said. 'A hundred times, yes. I mean, how many different ways could that ride have gone wrong, Veronica. And if you and I had died in there—'

'Died? Who dies on a roller coaster?'

'—if we had died in there, Veronica, think of how much in life you would have missed out on. And all because you were afraid, or because you were playing by someone else's rules about what you were allowed to do as a teenager, or as a girl, or as a boy who liked boys.'

'You're a weirdo,' she'd said. But the truth was that, even back then, she'd thought he might be right. There had always been so much to be afraid of in their family. Fear seemed to be the motivating factor in every decision their parents made. And she wasn't sure she wanted to live like that. She wanted to be rid of fear in the same way that he appeared to be. Or, well, if not in exactly the same half-crazed way, then in some way, in some other way.

And yet, here she was, twelve years later, still quivering.

From behind her, Michael said, "So it's that Space Mountain fills you with a Zen-like sense of peace, is that it?"

"I was just thinking," she told him. "Did you know that the summer before Matt came out to the family, he came out to me?"

"I always figured that you knew before the rest of us," said Michael.

"It was after we rode Space Mountain," said Veronica.

"Well, listen," said Michael, "I hate to break it to you, but I kinda figured out the truth about you and Desiree a long time ago. You know, even if you've never come right out and said it, a straight girl can only go to so many Ani shows before she's a gay girl."

Veronica smirked back at him.

"So, you're hoping what?" said Michael. "That you'll somehow find the courage to run away with Des just as soon as we're done here? That she and you will take Tracy and go hide away in some lesbian coven in Idaho or some damned place?"

"I'm not sure Idaho is the first place a group of gay girls would think of to hide out."

"Why not? All those potatoes..."

"Potatoes?" said Veronica, not following.

"All natural, easy to carve, come in all different sizes..."

Veronica laughed. "Cuz, you've got problems."

"Hey," he said. "apparently, it runs in the family."

She sighed. "I have the divorce papers in my purse, Michael. Or, well, Desiree has them, because she's got my purse. And I kind of figured that if I was ever going to find the courage to sign on the dotted line, it might be here."

"Oh," said Michael. "Well then, I'm gonna get out and push, because there is no way I'm letting them give you enough time to change your mind about this."

Veronica reached a hand back toward him, as far as it would go.

"Are you trying to hit me?" asked Michael.

"Grab my hand, idiot," she said, and he did.

She squeezed his hand, said to him, "It's going to be hard for Tracy, without a dad around."

"The Runt was never much of a father to begin with," he said.

"Do you think," said Veronica, "that you...?"

"What about Matt?" said Michael.

"He's got his own issues to deal with," she said.

"Father figures are overrated," said Michael. "Two women, you guys'll do it much better."

"But," said Veronica. "If she needs someone."

Michael squeezed her hand back, but didn't say a word.

The overhead lights went off with a quick flash.

"Oh boy," said Michael. "Here we go."

"You know what to do, right?" said Veronica.

"No," said Michael. "What?"

"When this thing gets going, you've got to scream. You've got to scream your damned lungs out."

"Ah, but the people who scream on these things—"

"Don't be judgmental, Michael. Give it a try. Scream like there's no tomorrow. Scream like you have nothing to lose. And then just scream because you feel like screaming."

"Okay," said Michael.

"Ready?" said Veronica, pulling her hand back. The tunnel of blue light began to pulse again.

"Sure," said Michael.

"Hands in the air?"

"Okay," he said.

The train slipped forward, down the hill. Light and sound pulsed around them. And then, as they rocketed forward into the darkness, they began to scream.

And it felt good.

THE SILVER FAMILY SINGERS

The one constant was music.

Whether it was my mother and her guitar, my uncle and his band, or that old record that my great-grandfather made back when he was as young as I am now—whatever it was, and whatever it sounded like, there was always music. In that house on the windswept shore of Harwich, it seemed as if life really did have a soundtrack. Through all of the ups and downs—Mom's divorce, Gramma's, the kerfluffle between Uncle Matt and Grampa over the deed—there always seemed to be a song drifting out of the background. The waves rolled in off of Nantucket Sound, leaving a wasteland of seashells in their wake. And Mom and I walked among them, me pinching my nose and asking what happened to the creatures who had once called these husks home, she humming a song in response, something she'd made up on the spot, something about how each of these shells was like a dream deferred, deferred and deferred and deferred again, until the dreamer was dead and gone and could no longer make good on the promise they'd made to themself.

So, there was always a song, even at the bleakest of times. In fact, in putting this compilation together, I've discovered that almost every song my family committed to a recording, regardless of how cheery the end-result may have sounded, actually grew out of a dark moment, a moment where despair threatened to shuck the songwriter's soul right out of his worthless hide. That each of these songwriters survived that assault and lived to tell the tale is a testament both to music in general, and to the songs they wrote in particular.

It does seem silly to me to be writing this when legal entanglements have made it uncertain that the compilation will ever see the light of day—Grampa wants his father's salty old jazz number sanitized, while Uncle Michael is demanding an unexpurgated version—but I suppose this is what you're talking about, Mrs. Sawyer, when you preach to us in class about writing for yourself first and foremost, and worrying about whether other eyes will see a work later on.

So, here goes. Here are one girl's thoughts on the songs that have been the background music of my life. Here are my notes on *The Silver Family Singers*.

"Mama Never Told Me My Porkchop Had a Name (It Was Philip)"
Words and music by Elijah Silver
Performed by The Eli Five
Recorded July 1931 in Chicago

RECORDED during a midwestern tour in the summer of 1931, when my great-grandfather Elijah Silver was just seventeen years old, "Mama Never Told Me" was released as the B side of a split disc with the Eli Five's tourmates at the time, The Bass River Trio. How those two Cape Cod-based outfits managed to find the cash for studio time when they could barely afford one square meal a day is the stuff of legend—all Gramp would ever say is that favors of "an adult nature" were provided to the studio owner by the Trio's lead singer and pianist, Marley Brown—but the real story, the one I'm interested in, is the story behind the song.

Eli's son, Robert, shudders at the thought that this song, laden with sexual innuendo, might come to be his father's lasting legacy. And, after all, he might have a point about it not being representative of the man we all grew up knowing or hearing stories about, a man so careful with his words that he needed to call an affair between consenting adults "an exchange of favors of an adult nature." But I think that Robert is missing the point, and that Michael Silver, Eli's grandson, is the one who truly understands what's going on.

"This song is about the man we all once were," said Michael in a December 2008 interview. "It's the story of a young man—a boy, really—who's just had his heart broken by an older woman, a woman who should have known better. And if he gets a little risqué in his lament, so be it. Boys, as they say, will be boys."

The lines at the center of the controversy come from the first verse: "My baby works down at the meatpacking plant / and she works every inch of meat that she can." And while that lyric leaves quite a first impression, the song never gets much worse than that when it comes to being risqué. Still, Robert Silver says that's more than enough. "That song is not who my father was, not who he ever was."

Robert's point, it seems—seeing as he doesn't want to ban the song from the collection outright—is that the instrumental is more representative of his father than the lyrics ever were, or ever could be. And, in that opinion, he is not altogether alone. The blistering conversation that takes place between Eli's trumpet and Dave Ford's saxophone captures the heated-yet-hilarious argument at the center of this piece perfectly. But there are those of us who think that the lyrics do add something, and there are those of us who do not, and whether this collection ever sees the light of day will have a lot to do with whether or not we can resolve this argument of the present, this disagreement that might best be settled, like the arguments of the past, with a pair of horns. Whoever runs out of breath first loses? I wonder what they'd say.

༻✿༺

"Sing, Angel. Sing."
Words and music by Veronica Silver
Performed by Veronica Silver
Recorded August 1999 in Boston

MY MOTHER, Veronica Silver, is best known in our family for her ability to take any song you throw at her, no matter how peppy or upbeat, to rearrange it for voice and guitar, or voice and piano, and to make it sound like a somber Sarah McLachlan tune. Take, for example, her plaintive covers of Ini Kamoze's "Here Comes The Hot Stepper" and George Michael's "Freedom '90," both of which appear elsewhere on this album. But, for all her success with tongue-in-cheek covers, she has struggled throughout her adult life with writing original material. Even when she does force songs out of herself, as she did during her stint at Berklee, she promptly deletes them from existence, erasing tapes, wiping out hard drives, swearing to silence those privileged few who have had the opportunity to hear her work.

The lone surviving example of her original material—she hasn't picked up her guitar in several years—is a bootleg that I myself made with a Fisher-Price tape recorder when I was just six years old. "Sing, Angel. Sing." is an improvised lullaby, the sort of thing she was constantly cooking up for me at bedtime. During my childhood, it was rare that a week went by when I didn't manage to convince Mom to bring her ukulele to my bedside at least once. The perks of being the only child of a loveless marriage, I guess.

I can still recall how my hands sweat as I clutched my little plastic tape recorder to my chest under the covers on that hot August evening. I was turned away from her, so that she wouldn't realize what I was up to. And I was more concerned with how well the recording was going to come out than with listening to the words she was singing, the notes she was plucking from her instrument. When I listen back to this recording—cleaned up by Mom as a sixteenth birthday gift to me just last year—I actually get that feeling of, "Boy, I wish I'd been there for that." It's silly, but it's true.

"Sing, Angel. Sing." isn't the best of the lullabies she made up for me during the Boston years, the years before my father left, but it's melancholy lyrics about singing even when everyone tells you to stop are indicative of her long-lost oeuvre, and of the woman she was then, a woman who wanted her daughter to be free in a way that she imagined she never would be.

❧

"Here Comes the Hotstepper"
Written by Ini Kamoze, Chris Kenner, Kenton Nix,
Salaam Remi
Arranged and Performed by Veronica Silver
Recorded December 1994 in Boston

FOR HER VERSION of Ini Kamoze's 1994 hit "Here Comes the Hotstepper," Veronica Silver imagines herself as not just a lyrical gangster, but as literal gangster, a hitwoman fighting her inner demons. In the chorus, when her background singers take over, she repeats, at the end of each line, the refrain of "murderer"—almost unintelligible in the original—so clearly, and with such venom, that the listener can't help but feel pity for this woman, this woman who is tearing herself apart from the inside out. Her crew sings her praises—"Here comes the hotstepper / She's the lyrical gangster / Excuse us, Mister Officer / Still laughin' like that" —and all the singer can do is lament how she got to where she is, and how little she is looking forward to where she's going.

Never a fan of rap music, or of all of the posturing she saw from its performers, she opened a performance in April 1997, her final year at Berklee, with this cover, dedicating it to the recently deceased Tupac Shakur and Notorious B.I.G. To say that her emphatic repetition of the lines "No, no, we don't die / Yes, we multiply" didn't go over well with the crowd would be an understatement. In an interview I conducted with her just last month, she admitted that the performance lacked tact, but she also seemed determined to clarify her intentions.

"I played it because I was afraid. I was afraid that these two murders were going to lead to more murders, and more music about murders and murdering people. And that's what that performance was about. If we kept churning out one violent act after another, we were going to be in trouble."

Controversy aside, my mother's version of "Here Comes the Hotstepper" is a noteworthy and amazingly different take on infectious song. And perhaps, once you've listened to it, you will find this version hard-to-resist as well.

☙❧

"Freedom '90"
Written by George Michael
Arranged and performed by Veronica Silver
Recorded May 1998 in Boston

VERONICA SILVER'S obsession with George Michael's "Freedom '90" has more to do with Christy Turlington than it does with George Michael. You'll remember, of course, that the singer refused to appear in the music video. In his stead, a series of supermodels were filmed in various states of undress, each of them mouthing the words to the song. And among those super-models, of course, was Ms. Turlington.

"How many times did I watch that video..." mused Veronica in my February 2009 interview with her. "It must've been nearly a hundred times that first year it was out, back when I was still coming to grips with who I was, with what I was. God, Christy was so intoxicating in it, walking across that room, bedsheet clutched to her otherwise naked chest, the train of it trailing behind her like some sort of gown. It was the video that did it for me at first. The song, not so much. I actually remember watching it on mute at least a time or two."

It was until George Michael was outed several years later that my mother went back and listened to the words, really listened to them. And that was where her version of the song grew from, that reinterpretation of the lyric as a description of the struggles of someone in the closet. She took the piano line, recast it in a minor key, and changed the gender of the song's auditor from male to female. And thus was born the other Veronica Silver classic.

"It's really insane to me," says Silver, "that I never caught on to the lyrics, not until he was caught in the bathroom. It was all like a frying pan to the forehead. How did I miss the meaning of 'There's something deep inside of me / There's someone I forgot to be'? I mean, 'Duh?,' right?"

The meaning may have escaped her early on, but my mother's version of the song demonstrates that, once she got the meaning, she *really* got it. Listen as she sings "All we have to do now / is take these lies and make them true somehow" and tell me that the cracking in her voice doesn't betray a deeper understanding of these words than George Michael's original. There are bits of awkwardness—her changing "buddy" to "hubby" in the line "Heaven knows we sure had some fun boy / what a kick just a buddy and me" is necessary to complete her recasting of the song as a goodbye to my father, but clumsy in its execution—but, all in all, this is a song of personal transformation for Veronica Silver. When she recorded it, she wasn't just singing about changing her life; she was in the midst of *actually* changing it. And that gives her version a sense of power that the original will forever lack.

☙❧

"Mistake"
Words by Michael Silver
Music by Robin Gates, David Johnson, and Billy Mills
Performed by Gideon's Bible (feat. Veronica Silver)
Recorded August 1995 in Malden, Massachusetts
Additional recording and production: September 1995 in Boston

WHILE THEY WOULD GAIN most of their notoreity as a three-piece, following the departure of David Johnson from the band in the summer of 1996, it could be argued that the true genius of Gideon's Bible is most easily found in the songs on the demo tape they recorded as a four-piece prior to Johnson's resignation.

"Mistake," the lead track on that three-song demo, was a Michael Silver composition, and the only one of the three songs that did not deal directly with the romantic dilemma faced by the three sides of the band's Fleetwood Mac-ian love triangle. That is not to say it was without controversy, however. On the contrary, it was just as controversial, if not more, in our family, for its portrayal of Michael's aunt and uncle, my grandparents, as irresponsible children who had no business being parents. Without ever explicitly naming names, Michael sings a lyric so biting and so caustic that it is surprise to this writer that this song has not held up the release of this compilation in the same way that The Eli Five's "My Mama Never Told Me" has.

I submit the first two verses for your inspection:

His mama was a whore
His daddy fought the war
Married, and then divorced
Just like everyone

Nineteen seventy-one
They heard the starter's gun
Just out to have some fun
Just like everyone

"Mistake" is also notable for its guest appearance by Veronica Silver on rhythm guitar, making it the only recording to date of two Silvers playing on the same song. Following a disastrous two-day long session with a disinterested producer at a ramshackle studio in the slums of Malden, the band visited Veronica Silver at Berklee to finish the tape. Veronica salvaged the band's exceptional performances from the reels and found the set lacking in only one area. "Mistake," she thought, sounded too sparse. And so, she stepped into the booth and added a rhythm guitar part to the intro, the choruses, and the outro (leaving Johnson's driving bassline and Gates's quick guitar hits to do he heavy lifting in the verses). The result is nothing short of the perfect opening track, an onslaught of angst and distorted guitars that would have made any Seattle native proud.

In later years, with Michael struggling to keep up with the fantastic bass parts David had left behind for him, and with Robin always feeling a bit inferior to her boyfriend's guitar-playing goddess of a cousin, the band had a hard time playing this song live. Each of the four instrumental parts were crucial to the whole, and they were never quite able to capture the magic on stage.

"Precious Whore"
Words by Robin Gates
Music by Robin Gates, David Johnson, and Billy Mills
Performed by Gideon's Bible
Recorded August 1995 in Malden, Massachusetts
Additional production: September 1995 in Boston

ON THE DAY that their tumultuous relationship began, Robin Gates and Michael Silver attended a Nine Inch Nails concert at the Worcester Centrum, and one of the songs that Trent Reznor and company performed that evening was the track "Reptile." The title of Gates's contribution to the original Gideon's Bible demo tape was taken from a line in that very song, and it is an apt description of how Robin saw herself, and of how many others saw her too.

The only relationship Robin Gates had that ever really lasted was the relationship she had with her guitar. Though she and Michael were "together" from January 1995 through January 1998, her wandering eyes and experimental personality kept that romance from ever being truly monogamous. She lived by a single law that applied to both her life and to her music. "I'll try anything once," she once said (in an interview with the *Phoenix*). "Twice if he's cute. And three times if it feels gooooodddd."

"Precious Whore" is centered around a blistering minute-long guitar solo that calls to mind both Kirk Hammet's work on the Metallica song "One" and Slash's gorgeous guitar line from the middle of "November Rain." Essentially meant to represent the orgasm of eponymous whore—it begins just after the line cribbed from Liz Phair, "I come when called"—Veronica Silver, whose work on the six-string actually intimidated Robin, said in my February 2009 interview with her that the Gates solo on "Precious Whore" made her cringe with jealousy. "She had to have felt that in order to play that," said my mother. "And, not to get too personal, but I was envious for more than one reason."

Guitar solo aside, the song is weaker in some ways than the song it shares the A side of the demo with—"Mistake"—and the song that follows it on the B side, "A Toast to the Duplicitous." Silver and Johnson were both much more accomplished lyricists than Gates, and a tendency to rely on lines cribbed from other songs further weakened her already predictable words. But the real story of this song is in the music. Everything that Robin Gates couldn't express in words alone comes out sounding crisp and clear when she uses her instrument as an interpreter. We don't need brilliant lyrics to understand the pain and pleasure of involved in being a city's "premiere rock and roll slut" (as she once described herself). It's all there in the solo, and in the riffing leading up to it.

⚜

"A Toast to the Duplicitous"

Words by David Johnson

Music by Robin Gates, David Johnson, and Billy Mills

Performed by Gideon's Bible

Recorded August 1995 in Malden, Massachusetts

Additional production: September 1995 in Boston

FEW PROFESSIONAL BANDS can pull off an eight minute rock song, and for a high school band the idea sounds simply preposterous, but the truth of the matter is that "A Toast to the Duplicitous," which takes up the entire B side of the Gideon's Bible demo tape, is one of the best eight minute rock songs this writer has ever heard. And that's probably because it was written by a high school band.

The trouble with the epic rock song is that it is, by it's very nature, over-the-top. Only a certain breed of performer seems authentic when singing or playing it. Meat Loaf can do them, because he is more an operatic or theatrical talent than a rock singer. Zeppelin can pull it off because, well, they're Zeppelin. And Skynyrd—well, the jury's still out on Skynyrd, isn't it? But a high school garage band (or basement band, as the case may be) playing an eight minute song? Now, there's an interesting dilemma.

On the one hand, a high school band shouldn't be able to sustain a listener's interest for that long. They just shouldn't. But, on the other hand, who better to compose an eight-minute musical melodrama than a person whose every day is melodramatic?

There are three distinct sections of nautically-themed "Duplicitous," one for each of the members of the band's love triangle. It begins with a lyrical assault on Michael set to what sounds like a melancholy Irish folk song. Here's a choice passage:

> You come from a long line of liars,
> a long line of thieves,
> drifting aimlessly
> across the sea.
> Your rudder is broken.
> The first mate is dead.
> You call yourself captain,
> but you're the only one left.

It continues, after further verses reference The Cars's "Best Friend's Girl" and The Beatles's "Rocky Racoon," with an attack on Robin that's set over a dark arrangement that clearly borrows from the heavier parts of "I Want You" (from *Abbey Road*). And it ends with haunting piece of self-critique, sung over what sounds like an attempt (and a surprisingly successful one at that) to blend the atmosphere of *Disintegration* (particularly the title track and "Fascination Street") with Kirk Hammett's *Black Album*-era solos.

The ambition here is beyond measure, and the fact that the band was ever able to pull this off, even once, is to be commended. But wouldn't it have been nice to see it live, to see if they could pull it off again? Those who followed the band during the height of its popularity will remember that it was never performed in concert, that the band deemed it "unplayable" in their famous 1997 interview with the *Globe*. But I will leave you with this nugget: this song *has* been played live, just once, in April 2001, at the joint bachelor/bachelorette party for Michael Silver and his bride-to-be Jenna Worthing. The three-person line-up performed it as an encore to a blistering live set with the help of Veronica Silver on guitar. And though it would have been something else to see the song sung by the man who wrote it—David Johnson, you will recall, dissolved the original version of the band and was never asked the rejoin when the other three reformed it —seeing it all was a once-in-a-lifetime event. If you scour the right corner of the Internet you might even be able to find a video of it, shot by a then eight-year-old fangirl with an unsteady hand.

"Go Your Own Way"
Written by Lindsey Buckingham
Arranged and performed by Gideon's Bible
Recorded live at the 1995 Chelmsford High School
Talent Show

THE PINNACLE of success for the four-piece version of Gideon's Bible was their performance at the 1995 Chelmsford High School Talent Show. The plan, early on, had been to attempt a live version of "Duplicitous," something that would really demonstrate the depth and breadth of their musical talent. But, as I've noted previously, it just didn't work outside of the studio. And so, an alternate plan was hatched.

Perhaps inspired by the Seaweed cover version found on the *Clerks* soundtrack, or perhaps not, Michael Silver, the biggest pop music fan in the group, lobbied hard for them to cover Fleetwood Mac's "Go Your Own Way." Singer David Johnson was against this from the start, and was only swayed when Robin Gates joined Michael to team up against him. Billy Mills, as always, remained indifferent on the issue. He would play whatever they wanted him to play.

Michael's campaign for the song was based around a sense of self-awareness that few young bands possess. He realized that, for their fanbase at the high school, Gideon's Bible was as much (if not more) about the soap opera as it was about the music. They were, in effect, CHS's own miniature version of the Mac. And he wanted to play off of that.

The recording of this song, borrowed from the audio of a video camera set up to capture the event, demonstrates just how successful Michael's gambit was. The band should not have been hailed for playing a song that was nearly twenty years old, except maybe by the adults standing watch in the shadows of the auditorium. But they were hailed, almost from the first note. The kids in that room may or may not have known the song before they walked into the concert that night. But they knew all they needed to know about what was to come, as soon as they heard those first lines: "Loving you / isn't the right thing to do." This was a band poking fun itself while, at the same time, rocking the roof off of that space.

A photo taken of Michael and Robin during the gig shows them singing into the same microphone, David off to one side, head down, plucking away on his bass. Michael and Robin are wearing serious rock and roll faces, playing the roles of conflicted lovers, but you can see smiles cracking through those masks. You can see that they weren't yet singing the song at each other, but were instead, at this point, singing it at David.

"You can go your own way / go your own way"

And that's just what David did. Over the summer that followed, they'd record their three-song demo and go on to somewhat great fame in the Merrimack Valley. But, within a year, David would disband the group—they would reform just a week after that, but things were never exactly the same—and the tension which had been the source of so much of their creativity would finally break them apart.

"Two Roads Diverging"
Words by Michael Silver
Music by Robin Gates and Billy Mills
Performed by Gideon's Bible
Recorded May 1997 in Concord, Massachusetts

and

"Mistress or the Muse"
Words by Robin Gates
Music by Robin Gates and Billy Mills
Performed by Gideon's Bible
Recorded May 1997 in Concord, Massachusetts

IT WASN'T until nearly two years later that the band, now reconstituted as a three-piece and gaining notoriety in the Boston music scene, finally re-entered the studio. They recorded two songs for a seven-inch at the beginning of their summer break from college, with every intention of recording a full-length disc before the year was out. But the romantic tensions between Robin and Michael were reaching their apex and Billy, sick of the drama after years of dealing with it, was ready to tender his resignation. And so, the seven-inch was all that fans of Gideon's Bible got.

The first song, "Two Roads Diverging," was a composition by Michael, a punk rock take on the concepts present in Robert

Frost's "The Road Not Taken," with a slightly more romantic tinge. The second song, "Mistress or the Muse," was gloomy ballad penned by Robin that, musically speaking, seemed to call back to "Duplicitous." Lyrically, the songs were like mirror images of one another. Michael, smitten now, however chastely, with the college housemate that would eventually become his wife, was wondering which path he should tread. And Robin, frustrated by the fact that Michael's songs about her were more popular with listeners than her songs about him, was wondering if she would only ever be a muse, or if she could ever hope to be his equal. And, even if she were more than a muse, would she ever be more than a mistress? Would she—could she?—ever be his true love.

The songs are tight and pared-down to their essential parts. There are no overdubs, save for the vocals, and the music therefore has a very live feel. But you can tell that Gideon's Bible is running out of things to say here. The songs are really just expansions on concepts they'd already explored.

And yet, you savor these songs just as much as you savor the others, maybe more, because you know that this is it. After the band broke up, Michael gave up music and returned to his art. Billy Mills, while still a presence on the drum riser for numerous bar bands in the Merrimack Valley, hasn't ever expressed an interest in getting back to the big time. And Robin—well, we all know the tragic story of Robin Gates. Shot down outside of her apartment in 2006, she would never fully realize the potential that we all saw in her.

There was a moment, during their one-night-only reunion on the eve of Michael's 2001 nuptials, that I saw the three of them looking at each other, as Robin's guitar bled feedback into the room, announcing the end of the show... there was a moment when I looked at them and had reason for hope, reason to believe that they would play again, that they would record again, that there would be more of this glorious music that surrounded me as I came of age. But then, as quickly as that moment had come, it was gone. They gave each other hugs, handshakes. And they went their separate ways.

"You have to savor what you've got," my great-grandfather used to tell us. It's one of the only things I remember of him from those brief few years of my life when he was alive. My aunt and uncles tell me that he was full of nuggets like that, but that one is really the only one that matters to me.

You have to savor what you've got, friends. Savor these songs. Listen to them, and then listen to them again.

Tracy Silver
Harwich, Massachusetts
March 23, 2009

ACKNOWLEDGEMENTS

These stories, with the exception of "The Seventh Draft" and "The Tale of Old Silas," first appeared in slightly different form on the Website echristopherclark.com. "The Tale of Old Silas" first appeared in slightly different form in a chapbook distributed for Free Comic Book Day 2009, and then again in the Fall 2009 issue of *Commonthought*.

Thanks to Elissa Quinn for designing the original version of the book, and thanks to the folks who supported the early stages of its production with their generous financial contributions: Joyce Bettencourt, Bodhipaksa, Larry Clow, Jena Marie DiPinto, Leigh Montgomery, Mary Ann Spilman, Derek J. Steen, Randy Tompkins, and the laptop donor who wished to remain anonymous. Thanks also to Phil Kliger for creating the soundtrack to the story "The Silver Family Singers."

Thanks to the writers who have mentored me over the years: David Crouse, Michael Lowenthal, Christina Shea, Tony Eprile, Rachel Kadish, and Steven Cramer.

Thanks to the members of the fiction workshops I was a part of during my time as a student in the MFA program at Lesley University, most especially to Shera Palmer Cook, Sara Oliver Gordus, Scott McCabe, and Jill Vora. Your assistance in crafting the early versions of some of these stories was invaluable.

Thanks to my colleagues at Lesley, most especially to Christopher Bock, Christine Evans, and Robert Wauhkonen. And thanks to my students at the university, both past and present.

Thanks to my former colleagues at the Association of Literary Scholars, Critics, and Writers, most especially to Michael Gouin-

Hart, Leslie Harkema, Richie Hofmann, Lisa Grove, Chelsea Bell, Beth Stone, Sean Gordon, Mike Russoniello, Erin McDonagh, Liza Katz, Katherine Hala, Tonya Serra, Rosanna Warren, Tom Clayton, Morris Dickstein, Christopher Ricks, Clare Cavanagh, Susan Wolfson, Greg Delanty, William Flesch, Tim Peltason, David J. Rothman, Rachel Hadas, Willard Spiegelman, Helaine Smith, Marcia Karp, Sarah Spence, Don Share, Peter Campion, Alex Effgen, and Zachary Bos.

Thanks to my former colleagues at JitterJam: Dave Brunette, Margaret Donnelly, Karen Grimmett, Tim Jones, Judi Mitchell, Matt Pierson, Ric Pratte, Jim St. Jean, and Marty Watts.

Thanks to all of the friends I've made at New Hampshire Media Makers, All Things Out Loud, Social Media Breakfast New Hampshire, PodCamp New Hampshire, and the various events I've attended and participated in at Studio 99 in Nashua, but most especially Avishay Artsy, Kevin Baringer, Michelle Boncek, Emily Briand, Jon Briggs, Chris Bujold, Tracy Lee Carroll, David Chevalier, Jeremy Couturier, Leah Creates, Carla Companion, Dan Freund, Chuck Galle, Roger Goun, Justine Graykin, Larry Graykin, Amy Greenlaw, Danielle Herman, John Herman, Sean Hurley, James Patrick Kelly, Nicole Kliger, Wayne Kurtzman, Shawn Lampron, Eric L'Ecuyer, Elise MacDonald, Christine Major, Jeanné McCartin, Kirk Membry, Kevin Micalizzi, Amanda Narcisi, Brian Paul, Lisa Peakes, Nick Plante, Leslie Poston, Bill Rogers, Alicia Staley, Brian Sullivan, P.T. Sullivan, Tara Sullivan, Jillian Thiele, Brian Turnbull, Matt Turner, Bryan White, and Scott Yates.

Thanks to the readers of and contributors to *Geek Force Five*. And thanks especially to my *Generation Goat* conspirator and long-time friend Jonathan Martin.

Thanks to friends who didn't fit into any of the categories above: Jimmy Arrington, Bryan Ballinger, Garen Boghosian, Corey Cook, Rachael Cook, Kay Coughlin, Heather Davis, Dan Del Rossi, Andy Hicks, Beth Jean, Stephen Jean, Monica Johnson,

Stacey Kerrigan, Crystal Lisbon, Brendan Mahan, Deb McCullough, Scott Mortimer, Beth Musser, Erik Paul, Jason Prokowiew, Julie Rattendi, Tori Ryan, Zeke Russell, Louann Santos, Jonathan Schlaffer, Bethany Snyder, Scott Spilman, Gradon Tripp, and Greg Tsiatis.

Thanks to family: Earl Clark, John Clark, Josephine Clark, and Susan Clark. And thanks to my in-laws: Anisa Woodsum, Liam Alexander, Julee Applegarth, Alex Cunningham, Artemas Foster, Mike Foster, Sam Foster, Nathan Woodsum, and Lesley Woodsum.

And, lastly, thanks to everyone I forgot, all of whom I now owe a drink.

ABOUT THE AUTHOR

E. Christopher Clark is the author of the Stains of Time series, a family saga with a hint of magical realism and a whole lot of time travel. His other books include the short story collections *Out of the Woods* and *Under the World*, the novella *The Seven Wives of Silver*, and a collection of poems cheekily titled *Bad Poetry Night*. His short stories have been published in *Live Free or Ride: Tales of the Concord Coach*, *River Muse: Tales of Lowell & the Merrimack Valley*, and the University of Hawaii's *Vice-Versa*. A graduate of Lesley University's MFA in Creative Writing program, he lives in Mass-achusetts with his wife and daughters.

echristopherclark.com

facebook.com/eccbooks

x.com/eccbooks

instagram.com/eccbooks

goodreads.com/eccbooks

pinterest.com/eccbooks

amazon.com/E.-Christopher-Clark/e/B00H0G94T0